COMING HOME TO INISHBEG

IZZY BAYLISS

For Lila, Tom, Bea & Charlie – my heart and my home.

1

PENNY

Leaving Dublin earlier had been like a dream. I still couldn't believe I had done it. Hot tears burned in my eyes as I moved around Lucy's room in a frenzy, grabbing whatever was nearest to hand and packing it into a small suitcase. Had it really been me who had, with trembling hands, put the case into the boot of the car then strapped our three-year-old daughter into the back seat? As I reversed out of the driveway, his cruel words still ringing in my ears, I didn't look back at the house. I didn't dare. I didn't know where I was going. I didn't have a destination in mind; I just knew that, at that moment, I needed to get as far away from him as possible.

I drove on autopilot through the maze of chaotic, traffic-filled suburbs that surrounded our home. Lucy sang along to the songs on the radio, oblivious to the pain I was feeling. My heart physically ached, as if my husband had taken it in his bare hands and twisted it until it was wrung dry. Tears spilled down my face and I couldn't seem to stop them.

I kept going and soon found myself on the motorway. Fields whizzed past in a blur of green, and I realised that the singing coming from the back seat had stopped. I glanced in the rear-view mirror to see that Lucy had fallen asleep. Her head was tilted to one side, her mouth was open, and her lips were damp with drool. Wild blonde curls fell around her face – curls she refused to let me brush, which made them altogether wilder. Pain seared through me. She looked so like him. Every time I looked at my beautiful daughter, she was a reminder of all that had happened.

After I had been driving for a while, my mind felt clearer. It began to whirr with questions. If Joe loved me, shouldn't he have begged me to stay? How had he let me walk out that door and take our daughter with me? Why hadn't he tried to stop me? It was almost as if he had wanted me to go ... but surely even he wouldn't want that? Would he?

After a couple of hours, I realised I had left the motorway far behind me and was climbing upwards on a narrow mountainous road – a road that, no matter how many times I drove along it, always made me nervous. I wiped away the tears that clouded my eyes. Although I knew the road well, it wasn't the kind of road you could let your mind wander on. I took a deep breath to soothe the panic that was coursing around my body and drove slowly, meeting each twist and treacherous bend with my heart in my mouth. My car climbed ever higher, seeking out the crest of the mountain until soon we were so high that a thick mist descended upon us and I had to switch on my fog lights. Eventually, the car snaked down the other side again and we finally emerged from the fog. I breathed a sigh of relief when I caught my first glimpse of the brooding ocean in the distance. Its ominous shade of navy blue was streaked silver where it met the sunlight on the horizon. The view never failed to take my breath away. My heartbeat began to slow. I was nearly home.

Soon we left the mountainous roads behind as the road lowered to sea level. The wind whipped through the grassy sand dunes on either side of me. I drove on until I saw the signpost marking the turn-off for Inishbeg Cove, and I felt the peculiar mixture of emotions I always felt about the village of my birth.

I could still remember my nervous anticipation all those years ago when I had left Inishbeg Cove to go to university in Dublin, aged eighteen. My tummy had been full of butterflies as Dad drove us out of the village that day. I knew I would miss my parents and the way the sea sparkled on a warm summer's day or how the water in the cove glinted orange just before dusk fell. Dublin seemed so far away – almost like another universe to me, a girl who had spent her whole life in Inishbeg Cove.

As I had slid my key into the lock of my student accommodation, eighteen-year-old me had felt heart-sore and overwhelmed. But after a few weeks of acute homesickness, I had discovered that Dublin life suited me. I loved the hustle and bustle of city life. I loved having so many places to go – there were endless cafés and bars right on my doorstep. The anonymity that Dublin offered was like freedom – everybody knew everybody in Inishbeg Cove. You couldn't walk for a minute without meeting someone you knew. People knew your business, even the things you thought were secret, but in Dublin nobody noticed me, let alone cared what I did.

Even now, after all this time, whenever I returned to Inishbeg Cove, the village always seemed smaller than I remembered, as if it had shrunk in my absence. Although it was always lovely to see my parents, I would usually start to miss the Dublin conveniences after a couple of hours, and I would breathe a huge sigh of relief whenever I was on the road back to the city again. So, to find myself driving towards Inishbeg Cove was something of a shock. It was as though the village was calling me home, the words carried on the sea breeze.

I rounded the sharp bend that led into the village, passing the *Welcome to Inishbeg Cove* sign that – for some reason – was decorated with bunting today. I went around by the old shipwreck and continued down the main street. More colourful bunting hung in zigzags outside the village hall; it looked as though there was a party taking place. I vaguely recalled Mam telling me about some celebration that was happening that weekend when I had spoken to her the week before, but I couldn't remember what it was for. I knew I was guilty of being wrapped up in my own life and not paying much attention to the village comings and goings that Mam was always so keen to share with me.

My parents' house was near the end of the main street, in a terrace of what had originally been fishermen's cottages. I pulled up outside, silenced the engine and felt my stomach flip-flop. What the hell was I doing here? What was I going to say to Mam and Dad? How would I explain it? They would be wondering why I hadn't told them I was coming. I checked my face in the mirror. My eyes were red-rimmed and the make-up I had applied that morning was a mess. I found a baby wipe in my bag and cleaned up my face, then I turned around to the back seat and gently roused Lucy.

'Wake up, baby girl. We're here.'

I watched her face slowly register where we were as she transitioned from the world of sleep. I climbed out of the car, unbuckled Lucy's straps and lifted her into my arms. Her breath was warm and comforting on my neck. I breathed in her sleepy scent mixed with briny sea air before walking up to the doorstep. I took a deep breath, pressed the doorbell and waited.

Mam flung open the door. 'Penny! What on earth are ye doing here?'

'Thanks for the warm welcome, Mam.'

'Sorry, love, it's just a surprise. Come on in.' She stood back to let us in. 'Why didn't you ring to say you were coming?'

My visit had clearly thrown her. Hell, it had thrown me; I hadn't expected to end up here either.

'Lucy, *a ghrá*, how are you?' my mother said as she took her out of my arms and cuddled her. I followed them into the kitchen.

'Hi-lo, Ganny,' Lucy said, and my mother beamed in adoration at her only grandchild.

'Well, you're after taking a stretch since I saw you last!' Mam turned back to me. 'Sure, it must be almost six months since ye visited.'

A wave of guilt floored me. Had it really been that long? My parents were getting on in years and I knew I should make the effort to visit more often. It was only then that I noticed Mam was wearing a turquoise dress with matching frock coat and an elaborate silver fascinator.

'You're very dressed up,' I remarked.

'I'm just heading out the door to the wedding.'

A wedding – that explained the bunting. The way she referred to it as 'the wedding' implied that I should know whose wedding it was but, although I racked my brains, I couldn't for the life of me remember who the couple were.

'Who's getting married?' I ventured.

'Honestly, Penny, do you listen to a word I say?' She

tutted in exasperation. 'I told you last week, Sarah O'Shea is marrying Greg the American.'

A-ha! I recalled listening to my mother telling me all about how Sarah had met the love of her life after he had travelled to Ireland in search of his ancestors, or something like that. 'Oh, is that today?'

My mother nodded. 'You should see them, Penny. They're love's young dream! There was Sarah, almost forty, all but given up hope of ever finding someone until Greg arrived here out of the blue. It just goes to show you' – she wagged her finger at me – 'no one knows what lies ahead for us. Love finds us, no matter how much you think you can hide from it.'

I felt my heart blister. Sarah was several years older than I was. Although I didn't know her well, I was glad she'd got her happy ending, but right now, this tale of true love and fate was like salt in my wound. I thought that had been my story once upon a time too. Tears filled my eyes, but I pushed them back. I didn't want Mam to see me upset.

'Greg is a lovely fella. Wait until you meet him, Penny!' Mam enthused.

I wasn't used to hearing my mam gushing so romantically, but it sounded like the whole village had been swept up in Sarah and Greg's love story.

'Where's Dad?' I asked.

'He's helping to set up the village hall for the reception afterwards. I'll meet him in the church. I do wish you had told me ye were coming, Penny...' Mam chastised me once again. 'I haven't even put fresh sheets on the bed for you.'

'We'll be fine, Mam.'

'I'm sure Sarah wouldn't mind if you and little Lucy came with us...' she continued.

I laughed. 'Mam, I'm not gate-crashing Sarah O'Shea's wedding. Lucy and I will be just fine here, don't worry.'

She still looked uneasy. 'And where's himself, anyway?'

Mam never called Joe by his proper name, instead always referring to him in the third person.

'Erm, he's working...'

'On a weekend?' Her brows hiked up into her forehead.

'He has a really important commission.'

She nodded half-heartedly and I knew she wasn't buying my story. 'He didn't come with you the last time you visited either,' she remarked through pursed lips. 'So how long are you here for?'

'A couple of days...'

'You really should have told me,' she repeated. 'I would have had a few treats and things for Lucy...' She trailed off.

'Don't worry about that stuff. Go and enjoy the wedding and tell Sarah and whatever his name is—'

'Greg.'

'Greg,' I repeated, 'that I said congratulations.'

'Are you sure yourself and Lucy will be okay by your-selves here?' she asked, tilting her head in concern.

'We'll be fine, Mam. Go on, go.' I forced myself to sound bright.

I watched my mother as she reluctantly turned to leave. I knew she suspected something was wrong, but how could I tell her what had happened? She'd only worry. Besides, I wouldn't be staying here for long. I was sure Joe and I would have patched things up in a couple of days. He just needed some space for a day or two. He would soon realise that he needed – *wanted* – us to come home.

2

SARAH

I had always thought I would feel differently on my wedding day. After all, I'd dreamed about this day since I was a little girl. As the years passed and I still hadn't found that special someone to share my life with, I assumed that dream had passed me by – but now, despite the odds, here I was, at the ripe age of forty-one, about to marry the love of my life. But instead of feeling excitement, anxiety was twisting a knot in my stomach ... and it was all because I was keeping a secret from Greg.

I should have told him. We were supposed to be starting married life together with a clean slate, not with secrets. I should have picked up the phone that morning as soon as I had found out, but telling him over the phone wasn't the right way to do it... I had thought about driving over to Cove View – the guesthouse owned by Greg's Aunt Maureen and her husband Jim, where Greg was staying because we were superstitious about seeing each other the night before our wedding – but I didn't want to bring bad luck our way. The thing was, I didn't know how he would react to my news, and what worried me most of all was that one look into his eyes would tell me everything.

I looked around at the whitewashed, lumpy stone walls of my bedroom and caught a glimpse of my reflection in the freestanding mirror in the corner of the room. My make-up had been carefully applied by Mrs O'Herlihy's granddaughter, Caoimhe, who was training to be a make-up artist in Limerick. I rarely wore make-up – there wasn't much call for it, sitting in the draughty post office in Inishbeg Cove – but Caoimhe was like a magician. The lines on my face had been softened and my skin looked more radiant somehow. I hadn't wanted anything fancy; I was no blushing bride, after all, but she had insisted on curling my blonde hair, so it fell in loose waves around my shoulders.

Greg and I were no spring chickens and neither of us liked being in the limelight, so we had agreed that a simple, low-key affair was exactly what we both wanted. When he had suggested we hold the reception in the village hall, it had felt perfect. We had put Tadgh in charge of the food, publican Jim was going to set up a bar, and Ruairí had offered to make the wedding cake. The *céilí* band that usually performed in the Anchor were going to provide the music. I had made the invitations myself and, although they weren't very sophisticated, I thought they had turned out rather well. We weren't having bridesmaids or best men, flower girls or pageboys; I hadn't wanted any fuss, although lord knew that many of the village women had tried to cajole me into choosing tasteful wedding stationery or looking at elegant floral arrangements. The wedding was really just going to be a shindig for the villagers and a few friends of Greg's who had made the trip over from North Carolina. Maureen would be there too, of course; she and Greg had grown close since the old secrets had finally been aired and time had allowed the wounds to heal, and we were thrilled that Greg's biological father Albie was able to make it too. Albie's multiple sclerosis had rendered him wheelchair bound, and he lived in a care home. Greg's birth parents had given him up for adoption within hours of his birth, and sadly his mother Della had passed away several days later. Although Albie hadn't been a part of Greg's life growing up, he and Greg had got to know one another over the last year. Greg visited him often and would bring him for a walk around the grounds of Grovetown Hospital, or some-times he would come to our house for dinner. I was so happy when Greg told me a nurse was going to accompany him to the wedding so he could share the day with us.

I picked up the black-and-white wedding photograph of my deceased parents from my windowsill. My mother was youthful and slender, her face aglow as she stared lovingly into my father's eyes and he looked adoringly back at her. He had movie-star good looks, a strong jaw and dark wavy hair. Together, they were such a glamorous couple. I traced my fingertip along their faces. How I wished they could be here with me today. I longed to ask my mother if she had felt jitters on the morning of her wedding. Had her stomach been in knots too, or had she been calm and content as she got ready to marry my father? They would have really liked Greg. He was a great person – I was so blessed to have found him. I just wish I had shared my secret with him before our wedding.

'Sarah, dear?' Mrs Manning called up the stairs to me. 'Come on down here! What on earth is keeping you? It's nearly time to go to the church. We need to get you into that dress. We don't want to keep Greg waiting.'

I could imagine Greg pacing at the altar, his brow creased with worry. I had promised him that I would be on time.

'I'm coming!' I called back to Mrs Manning, feeling the knot in my stomach pull tighter until I could barely breathe.

Mrs Manning had come to be a mother figure to me after my own mother had passed away several years back. She had been instrumental in Greg and me getting together. Although she was ninety-three and used a walking stick to get around, she was the only person I had wanted to walk me down the aisle.

I opened my wardrobe and lifted out the ivory lace column wedding dress that had been my mother's. It was boat-necked, with long sleeves. I'd removed a few ruffles to modernise it a little, but otherwise it was the same dress she had worn all those years ago. It gave me comfort to know that the delicate lace fabric had once touched her skin too, and I felt as if I was keeping her close to me on my wedding day.

'Are you okay, my love?' Mrs Manning asked, studying my face when I reached the bottom of the stairs. 'You're very pale. Maybe I'm just not used to seeing you with make-up on...'

She was dressed in a long ruby-red cardigan over a knitted lurex dress. With her fox-red hair and scarlet lipstick, she'd be the most glamorous guest at our wedding. Even in her nineties she was still a head-turner. How I wished I had confided in Mrs Manning, but I could hardly do it now.

'I feel a bit sick, actually...'

She clasped my hands between her own, which were covered in brown age spots. 'It's just nerves. You'll be fine once you see Greg.'

'Do you think so?'

She looked at me, puzzled. 'Of course I do. Now come

on, dear, it's time to get you into that beautiful dress. We don't want you to be late.'

She unzipped the dress with her shaky hands and held it out for me to step into. Then she turned me around and pulled up the zip.

'I remember your mother wearing this dress all those years ago too, Sarah,' Mrs Manning whispered as I turned to face her. 'You look just like her.'

Moisture filled her eyes, and I felt tears threaten.

'Don't!' the older lady warned. 'You'll ruin your make-up.'

She helped to place the veil on my head and adjusted it until it was in the right position. Then she moved back to admire me. 'Sarah O'Shea, you are a vision. Just wait until Greg sets eyes on you. Imagine, that's the last time I'll call you Sarah O'Shea. We'll all be calling you Sarah Klein from now on!' She clapped her hands together giddily.

Plump tears began to stream down my freshly made-up face.

'Oh my goodness, what's the matter?' Mrs Manning looked worried. 'It's only a name, Sarah, for heaven's sake! If you really don't want to change it, you can keep your maiden name ... loads of women do nowadays.' She tutted.

I shook my head. 'It's not that.'

'Well, what is then? You're not having second thoughts, are you, dear?'

She handed me a tissue and I dabbed my eyes. 'I don't think so...'

'It's just nerves, Sarah,' she counselled. 'Sure, it's only normal. I've never seen a couple more destined to be together than you and Greg – and I've had my fair share of men! Don't ruin this for yourself. It's okay to be happy.'

I looked at the clock on the wall, people would be

starting to arrive at the church. Greg was probably standing at the altar checking his watch nervously, wondering what was keeping me. Everyone was waiting on me; I couldn't drop the bombshell now.

'Come on, dear,' Mrs Manning urged. 'I can hear Tadgh outside with the car.'

I took a deep breath. It was time to go.

3

Through the living room window, I watched Mam as she disappeared down the path in the direction of the village hall. The sun shone brightly over the cove and the canvas of blue sky was patched with criss-crossing white vapour trails. Lucy was sitting on the floor by my feet playing with the Lego Mam kept in the house for her.

I picked up my phone and checked it once more, but my heart sank further when I saw that Joe hadn't tried to contact me. I had been hoping I had somehow missed a call or a message from him. Maybe he would offer me an explanation or even an apology. I had been replaying his last words to me over and over in my head: 'I need space, Penny. I think it's best if you go away for a while.' I was trying to make sense of it all but, no matter how much I tried, I couldn't understand why he was doing this.

Joe and I had been married for eight years, and I was used to his moods and behaviours. This wasn't the first time he had done something like this. He was an artist, with a reputation as one of Ireland's leading pop culture painters.

His work was known for its stark, and sometimes hideous, subjects, and he only used dark, brooding colour palettes. Once he had installed a festering tin of beans in our kitchen. Flies had crawled all over it and it stank, but he had refused to remove it until he had finished painting it.

I've never told anybody this before, but when Lucy was only a few weeks old Joe received a commission from a Chinese art collector. He was paid an exorbitant amount – the most he would ever receive for a piece of his art. He had left me alone with our new-born baby and moved into a hotel for a month, claiming he needed to be in the 'right headspace' to work.

I know it might sound perverse, but I had to admit that I had once found his strange foibles endearing, where others might not have been so tolerant. His intensity, his passion and the need to put his art above all else were awesome to witness. I guess it was his intense focus that attracted me to him in the first place. When he was in the zone, nothing could pull him out of it – I often wondered, if his studio went on fire while he was creating, would he even notice? He lost all awareness of time and his surroundings. There were even days when he forgot to come home and stayed working in the studio all night. He was like an actor who gets into character for a role by speaking like their character, dressing like them and even eating the same food as them. They immerse themselves so completely that you don't know where the character begins and the actor ends. That's what Joe was like: there was no separation between him and his art.

Friends of mine would listen, wide-eyed, whenever I shared snippets of my life with them, so I stopped telling people about our relationship. I never used to envy the mundanity of their lives: the long commutes to nine-to-five office jobs, maybe a shared bottle of wine on a Saturday night the only thing to look forward to. Where was the excitement in that? But lately ... lately, there were times – especially since Lucy had been born – when I yearned for something a bit more 'normal', a bit more like the family setting I had grown up with.

Although I would never admit it to anyone, if I was being really honest, for the past few months I had been struggling with Joe's need to put his art above everything else. It would be nice to not find his side of the bed empty night after night because he was working late in his studio. Or to be able to leave Lucy with him if I needed to go some-where, without being told that he couldn't be disturbed even for half an hour. But then I would remind myself that it was all part of the man I loved: I had known when I married him that life with Joe de Paor was never going to be conven-tional. I had to take the good and the bad, so that's why I was sure this morning's outburst was just another part of his creative process. He'd been overwhelmed by the artistic drama in his head.

I leant forward and brushed a stray curl off Lucy's fore-head, then got up and went into the kitchen. I flicked the switch on the kettle and listened as it grumbled to life. Suddenly my phone rang, and I rushed back to the living room, where I had left it on the coffee table. Hurriedly I picked it up but saw Dad's number on the screen instead of Joe's.

'Dad?' I said, a wave of disappointment flooding through me. 'Are you having a nice time at the wedding?'

'It's lovely, but Penny, your mother just told me you're down for a visit. Is everything okay?'

'Of course, Dad,' I lied.

He paused. 'Well, it's just that usually you tell us when you're coming home...'

'Sorry, I didn't realise I needed an appointment to visit my own parents!' I snapped, then regretted it as soon as the words had left my lips. I knew it was childish. Dad was just concerned. Hell, if Lucy turned up on my doorstep out of the blue in thirty years' time, wouldn't I be worried too?

'Now you know that's not how it is. We love having you, we wish you'd visit more often, if anything ... but it's just a bit ... unexpected. You would tell us if something was wrong, wouldn't you, love?'

'Of course I would, Dad. Sorry, I just thought it would be nice to surprise you both. Now stop worrying.'

'Okay ... well, we won't stay too late. We'll be home straight after the meal.'

'Don't leave early on my account. I'm fine – just enjoy the day.'

After I had hung up, I sat down at the table, feeling guilt eat me up. Why wasn't I able to tell them the truth? I knew a large part of me didn't want them to think badly of Joe. Although they had never said so out loud, I had always known that they didn't really like him. I used to think it was because of the age difference – Joe was thirteen years older than me. We had met when I was still in college. Back then he had called me his muse, said he couldn't work without me. We had moved in together after only three weeks. He'd said he couldn't make art unless I was present – he needed to eat, sleep and breathe me. At the time I couldn't understand my parents' concerns, but since I had had Lucy, I guess I could now see why they had been worried. They also never really 'got' his art. They couldn't understand why people would pay thousands for an image of a mouldy tin of beans or a plate of chips with ketchup smeared over them. 'Where's the beauty in that?' they had asked. Mam had once said, 'There's no accounting for taste.' I never did tell Joe that.

I was afraid that if I told them what had happened that morning, I would be proving them right. Besides, I still hoped this was all temporary. If Mam and Dad knew the truth, they'd always hold it against Joe. Even though Joe and I had our problems, I still loved him and couldn't bear for them to think badly of him. I didn't want to worry them and risk them disliking him even more, especially after we'd sorted things out and were ready to put our argument behind us. I was sure it was another example of the 'artist at work'. Knowing Joe, he would wake up tomorrow morning and beg us to drive back to Dublin, saying he couldn't work without his family. He would realise that this was a moment of madness and he needed Lucy and me at home.

4

SARAH

Through the car window, I watched the waves rise like seahorses as they raced towards the shoreline. As we neared St Brigid's church, Mrs Manning reached across the seat and gave my hand a tight squeeze.

'Nearly there now, my dear.'

Beads of sweat broke out across my forehead and I thought I might be sick all over my mother's wedding dress.

When we reached the church, Tadgh hopped out of the driver's seat and came around to open the rear door. Before he had even touched the handle, I pushed it open myself and rushed out past him to gulp down fresh air.

'Are you okay, Sarah?' he asked, tilting his head to the side. 'You're very pale...'

I nodded, not trusting myself to speak.

'Can't wait another minute to marry Greg, eh?' He laughed, and I smiled weakly.

He went around to the other side to help Mrs Manning out. Once she was steady on her stick, we set off towards the church.

When we appeared under the floral garland that framed

the arched doorway, there was a collective gasp. I had made the garland myself from the roses in Mrs Manning's garden, twined with ivy I had taken from the cottage walls. A breeze lifted my veil, which rippled out behind me on the wind. I heard Pachelbel's 'Canon in D' begin. It felt as though my stomach was filled with a million butterflies, careering around wildly inside me.

'Ready?' Mrs Manning said, turning to look at me.

I took a deep breath and gripped her arm and, with my heart thumping wildly, we began walking. My forehead and the back of my neck were damp and clammy. I was pretty sure that all the make-up that Caoimhe had carefully applied earlier was now running down my face.

The aisle felt excruciatingly long – even longer because we were walking at Mrs Manning's pace. It felt as though everyone's eyes were boring into me, and I couldn't help wondering if they had guessed my secret.

Eventually Greg's smiling face came into view at the altar but, instead of feeling excitement, my stomach heaved. I took a deep breath, willing myself to stay calm. When we reached him, Greg leant over and hugged Mrs Manning before taking my hand and whispering, 'You look beautiful. Ready to start the rest of our lives?' He grinned at me and my heart twisted.

'We are here today to celebrate the love of two very special people...' Father Byrne announced as he began our wedding ceremony.

As we listened to the readings and prayers, all carefully selected by Greg and me, my mind kept returning to the secret I was keeping from him. I was going to have to tell him today; I just hoped it wouldn't ruin our wedding day.

Suddenly I was being nudged gently. 'Sarah – the vows...' the elderly priest prompted. I realised with a start that I had been miles away. A ripple of laughter broke out among the guests. I quickly gathered myself.

'Er ... I, Sarah...' My voice trembled, and Greg smiled at me. '...take you, Greg, to be my husband, for better, for worse, for richer, for poorer, in sickness and in health, all the days of our lives.'

Greg squeezed my hand reassuringly.

'What God joins together, man must not separate. I now pronounce you husband and wife,' Father Byrne announced. A rapturous cheer broke out around the church.

Despite my worries, it was hard not to get swept up in the goodwill radiating from everyone. We went out into the churchyard, where the villagers showered us with confetti. The May sun shone brightly from the aquamarine sky, broken only by the wispiest of pulled candyfloss clouds. The sea twinkled in the cove and white fishing boats bobbed lazily, as if they were joining in on the merriment too.

We walked the short distance to the village hall. As we got closer, I saw that it had been transformed. Pastel-coloured bunting streamed down from the roof, sloping towards the ground in long, criss-crossing lines. In front of the hall, rows of spindly gold chairs were tucked neatly under three long tables, which were covered in white linen cloths. Vases blossomed with hydrangeas and the fuchsias that grew wild in all the hedgerows around the village. As I got closer to the tables I noticed that a simple wildflower decorated each place setting. I was truly speechless. I had left the decorating in Ruairí's capable hands, but this was beyond my wildest dreams. He had taken an ordinary parish hall and transformed it into a venue worthy of a magazine spread, with the cove as the perfect backdrop. Gulls screeched and caterwauled across the brilliant sky, chasing the fishing boats, and I felt a contentment that I was in my village, with all the people I loved around me. This was happiness. Then I remembered my secret.

'I told you we'd make it special,' Ruairí said, catching my eye and winking.

'You are amazing, thank you so much.' I planted a kiss on his cheek. 'I couldn't have dreamed of anywhere nicer.' Suddenly I was overcome by emotion.

'It was all the villagers' hard work,' he said modestly. 'We wanted everything to be perfect for you and Greg.'

We took our places and Tadgh treated us to a feast of shellfish and fillet steak with baby potatoes. There were crab claws, wild Atlantic cod, and the freshest garden vegetables. The food kept coming.

After we had finished eating, Greg stood up and tapped a spoon against his glass.

'I thought we weren't doing any speeches?' I whispered.

'I know, but today has been amazing. I feel I have to say a few words to thank everyone.'

'Okay.' I smiled at him as he stood up. I could tell he was nervous.

He cleared his throat and began. 'I wasn't going to make a speech, but as I look around at everyone here today – the most important people in our lives – how could I not? I just want to say thank you to everyone who put so much work into this day. From the ceremony to the décor to the food, it has been truly magical. I also want to thank my *wife* – God, it feels so good to say that...' He paused as everyone laughed. 'I just wanted to say that meeting Sarah was the moment my life changed forever. When I left North Carolina I was searching for my birth parents, but I found so much more. I found a father in Albie, I found a community that has welcomed me wholeheartedly, but I also found something I wasn't expecting. I met the woman I'd been waiting for my whole life, and a place to call home. I never thought I would say this but opening the letter from my parents ended up being the best thing that ever happened to me because it has brought so much goodness into my life. Thank you all, each and every one of you, for being with Sarah and me to celebrate today. It means so much to us both.'

I had to use my napkin to dab tears away. I just hoped he would feel the same way after I had told him.

After we cut the cake, a divine three-tiered affair decorated with the sweetest strawberries and freshly whipped cream, Greg and I had our first dance to 'Summer Wind' by Frank Sinatra. As the sun began to set over the cove, Greg twirled me beneath the twinkling fairy lights that Ruairí had hung around the exterior walls of the hall. We danced until the stars were out, twinkling like crystals studding the velvet sky above us.

After the céilí band had finished playing and we had said goodbye to most of our guests, I found myself hit by a wave of exhaustion. I sat down on the sea wall. The evening air had grown chilly and I couldn't help shivering.

'Is everything okay, wifey?' Greg said, placing his jacket over my shoulders. 'I don't think I'll ever get bored of saying that.'

'I'm just tired...' Almost on cue, a yawn escaped my mouth. Dusk was settling over the cove and it wouldn't be long before a heavy cloak of inky darkness fell over the countryside. In the distance, the yellow beam of the lighthouse sliced through the night sky, giving ships warning of the rocky promontories on the coast. The lights from the fishing villages that dotted the shoreline were like amber jewels threaded along a necklace. Just an hour ago the place had been alive with music, dancing and good cheer, but now only Greg and I remained, sitting on the sea wall. All of our guests were gone home, the fairy lights had been switched off, and the band were lifting the last of their equipment into their van.

'I like your thinking, Mrs Klein,' Greg said playfully. 'Let's go carry you over the threshold.'

My stomach flip-flopped. I knew the time had come to be honest with him. I couldn't put it off any longer.

I placed my hand on his arm and bit my lip. 'Greg...' I said tentatively.

'Yes?'

'I need to tell you something.'

His face clouded over. 'What is it?'

'I'm so sorry, I didn't mean for it to be today of all days ...'

'Okay, you're really scaring me now, Sarah. What's going on?'

'I swear I'm not trying to trick you, or start married life with secrets—'

'Sarah, will you just tell me what is going on, please?'

I took a deep breath, ready to finally share my secret with him.

The heavy thrum of the ocean had faded into a blur behind me and the bunting flapping in the evening breeze and the constant swell and roll of the sea as the waves broke along the shoreline were the only sounds to be heard.

'Sarah, you have to tell me what's going on,' Greg demanded, standing in front of me. He never usually raised his voice, but my behaviour had rattled him. I looked into his eyes, which were full of fear, and I knew I couldn't keep my secret from him any longer.

I had to tell him.

'I'm pregnant,' I blurted.

The fear in his eyes was replaced with disbelief.

'What? Are you sure?'

I nodded. 'I did a test this morning. My cycle is so irregular so at first I was convinced that my period was just late with the stress of organising the wedding but I've been really nauseous for a while now so I just said I'd do a test to rule it out. I nearly collapsed when it turned positive.'

Greg wasn't looking at me; instead, his gaze was fixed on

the black ocean behind me. His reaction was confirming my worst fears. What a way to start married life. A tear travelled down my face. I should have told him before the wedding.

'Please, say something, Greg,' I begged.

'It's just such a shock. I'm trying to get my head around it...'

'I'm so sorry. I just never thought at my age it would happen...' More tears pushed forward, and soon they were falling freely down my face. We had never discussed having children and because my cycle was so erratic, I assumed that my body was gone past it. What if he didn't want to have a baby? It felt as though all the happiness I had known for the last year was being wiped away.

Suddenly I felt his hand lifting my chin so that I looked into his eyes.

'Hey, what are you crying for? Unless I'm missing something, this is good news, right?'

'It is?'

'Of course it is! Why wouldn't it be? Are you trying to tell me that you don't want to keep our baby?' He frowned.

I shook my head quickly. 'Of course not! I could never do something like that but, well ... I'm forty-one...'

'Sarah, you crazy girl.' He grinned at me and put his hands on my shoulders, as if to steady me. 'It's a shock, I'll give you that, but to get a chance at my age to be a dad ... it's a dream come true.' Happiness flooded his face, and relief washed through me.

'I never thought we'd have children, Greg. I thought my body was past all that. You hear about women's fertility falling off a cliff once they hit forty. I never thought a baby would be an option for us.'

'I guess we're the lucky ones.' He beamed at me. 'God, I can't believe I'm getting a chance to be a dad – just when I thought life couldn't get any better! This is the icing on the cake. Marrying you here today in front of our friends and family and then to learn this news – this is like a dream!' Happiness shone from his eyes.

'But what about the risks, Greg?' I didn't want him getting carried away. It was easy to let ourselves get excited, but there was no escaping the fact that having a baby at my age was not risk-free. 'You know you hear about the risks on the TV and radio all the time. Down Syndrome or other chromosomal abnormalities, not to mention the risk of premature birth or the baby being stillborn—'

'Stop, Sarah.' He placed his index finger on my lip. 'We're on this path now together.' He put his other hand on my stomach. 'This baby has chosen us to be its parents and we need to step up to that. We'll take what we get. We'll roll with the punches, whatever life throws at us. It's our baby – we'll love it no matter what.'

I threw my arms around him, a sobbing mess.

'Maybe it's the hormones,' I blubbed, 'but I love you, Greg Klein. I mean, I really, really love you. When I set out this morning to marry you, I didn't think I could possibly love you any more than I already do, but I think you've gone up a whole level.'

Greg started to laugh, and I realised that everything was going to be okay. Why had I ever doubted him? It wasn't just about Greg and me any more; two were set to become three. As he wrapped me in the sanctuary of his broad arms, I knew that no matter what hurdles life threw at us, I had my husband by my side and we would take them on together.

6

PENNY

I saw every hour change on the alarm clock that sat on the table beside my bed. I had lain awake all night, my mind racing with worries as the light creeping around the edge of the blind changed from deep navy, to pinky-orange, until finally it was a bright morning white. I felt a kick in my abdomen, then another jolt in my neck, and realised it was thanks to the deadly combination of Lucy's heel *and* elbow. My three-year old had prodded me and kicked me all night long, leaving me clinging to the edge of the double bed we shared. She was lying horizontally now, her sweet face relaxed, lost in the land of nod. I loved watching her sleep, her small chest rising and falling reassuringly. Her mouth was half-open. How I wished that I could sleep the innocent sleep of a child.

I looked around my childhood bedroom. Yellowed Sellotape still clung to the walls from my teenage days, when I'd ripped posters of my teenage crushes out of magazines and quickly stuck them up, before pulling them down again in favour of someone new in the following week's edition. I could smell fried bacon. My stomach growled, and I realised

I hadn't eaten since breakfast the day before. Gently, I woke Lucy, scooping her up into my arms. She was still in that enchanting half-awake, half-asleep state, burying her warm face into my neck while I carried her down to the kitchen.

'Smells delicious, Mam,' I said, coming into the kitchen.

'Penny!' Dad stood up and gave me a hug. 'It's great to have ye home.'

I had been in bed before they had come home the night before.

'Sit down there, love.' Mam pulled out a chair for me. Lucy stayed on my knee, still cuddly and sleepy while Mam served up breakfast.

'How was the wedding?' I cut into the rasher, almost salivating. Nobody cooked a breakfast as good as Mam did.

'Ah, it was lovely – it would make you feel good about the world looking at the picture of happiness that Sarah and Greg are. They were made for each other.'

'Here, I'll hold her while you eat,' Dad said, putting his hands out to take Lucy. 'Come up here to Grandad, *a leanbh*.'

Dad cut up some bacon into small pieces and, even though Lucy was well able to feed herself, he speared them with a fork and fed them to her.

'So, how's Joe?' he continued. I knew he'd guessed that something was wrong and was subtly trying to bring up the subject.

'He's good, really busy at the moment,' I said, cutting into a sausage. 'He has an exhibition later in the year so he's flat out, getting ready for that.'

Mam pursed her lips in disapproval. 'I thought you said he was working on a commission?'

'He has that too—'

'So how long will you be staying?' Dad asked.

I twirled my fork between my fingers. 'A week, I think.'

'Well, take as long as ye need. This will always be your home.'

I felt a lump in my throat and tears in my eyes. It was as if they could see through my charade and knew that this wasn't an ordinary visit home. 'Thanks, Dad. I think I might take Lucy down to the beach after breakfast, but I didn't bring her swimsuit,' I said, changing the subject.

'You came all the way down to visit and forgot her swimsuit?'

I knew Mam was suspicious, but a swimsuit had been the last thing on my mind when I had been packing our bags.

'Sure, a pair of shorts and a T-shirt will do her grand,' Dad said.

AFTER BREAKFAST I set off with Lucy on the short stroll to the cove. As we walked down the main street, I saw that little had changed since my last visit. But things never did in Inishbeg Cove. O'Herlihy's had plastic footballs and bucket-and-spade sets hanging outside the window, trying to make the most of the summer season. I decided to go in and buy a set for Lucy.

'Well, if it isn't yourself!' Mrs O'Herlihy beamed as I entered the shop. 'I saw your mam and dad at the wedding last night and they told me you were home to visit all right.'

I wondered if my visit home had been the topic of the night, or maybe I was being paranoid.

'Little Lucy is getting big,' she went on.

'She is, Mrs O'Herlihy.' I knew I would have this same conversation approximately fifty times before the weekend was out. It was always the same whenever I came home.

One of the things I had loved when I moved to Dublin was not having to make small talk with everyone I met.

I paid her and continued on through the village. I passed Sarah's post office, although it was closed for the weekend. Someone had touchingly hung the same bunting used to decorate the village hall over the doorway.

As I walked, I saw that Ruairí's café had tables and chairs outside under the blue-and-white striped awning, and hanging baskets bursting with petunias and pansies brightened the wall on either side. Next door, the old butchers had been transformed into an ice-cream shop. That hadn't been there the last time I was home. A vintage-esque sign overhead read *Greg's Ice-cream Parlour*. I wondered if this was the famous Greg that Sarah had married. When I reached it, I peered in through the window. A long counter ran down the middle, with stools tucked beneath it, and a few booths hugged the wall like in a traditional ice-cream parlour from an old American movie. The facade had been painted calamine pink, adding a lovely splash of colour to the main street. Immediately Joe's mocking voice was in my head, saying, 'How twee.' I pushed it out quickly and kept walking.

Across the street the wedding bunting still decorated the village hall, and the pastel-coloured flags rippled gently in the breeze. I had spent so much of my childhood in the village hall at Irish dancing *feiseanna* or at my friends' birthday parties. It had even served as a temporary school when the roof had blown off Inishbeg Cove National School during a particularly violent storm. It was the last place I would have imagined being used as a wedding venue, but seeing it here on this glorious sunny day, decorated so prettily, I had to admit that it gave the minimalist Dublin hotel where Joe and I had married a run for its money.

Lucy and I headed for the path through the dunes that

led down to the cove. I inhaled the salty air deep into my
lungs, breathing in the smell of home that I loved, cleansing
my lungs of polluted city air. As I took off my sandals and
walked barefoot on the sand, I instantly felt my shoulders
start to relax; I really believed the air here had medicinal
qualities. A group of sea swimmers wrapped in towels stood
around chatting and drinking from thermos flasks. The sea
was calm, and waves broke gently on the shoreline before
sweeping along the rippled sand. Gulls screeched above us
as they scavenged the sand for creatures washed up by the
outgoing tide. Lucy ran along in front of me searching for
shells to put in the bucket I had bought in O'Herlihy's.

'Ook, Mama,' she called.

I walked over and bent down to look at the shell she
handed me. 'Wow, that's so pretty, Lucy.'

I stood back up and looked out to where a man was
paddling a surfboard. The waves were calm that day, so he
couldn't have been a regular surfer in chase of the foam. He
stood up when the water grew too shallow to paddle any
more and walked towards the shore, tucking his board
underneath his arm. As he got closer, I realised with a start
that it was Tadgh. I watched him as he waded through the
shallow water, oblivious to his audience. He was carrying a
crab in his other hand. I couldn't believe he still caught his
crabs by hand this way. He walked up the beach and put
the crab in his bucket that he had left on the sand. He
dropped his board and ran his fingers through his dark
hair, scattering water droplets everywhere. Before I could
stop her, Lucy had run over to him and was peering into his
bucket.

'What in there?' I could hear her ask.

'They're crabs,' he said.

I quickly followed her over, my heart racing.

'Penny?' Tadgh said, recognising me as I got closer. He was clearly as surprised as I was.

'Hi, Tadgh. I see you've taken on the family method of crab fishing.'

'What can I say? It's in the genes. God, I can't believe it's you. It must be – what? Twelve years since I saw you?' He shook his head, but his eyes stayed locked on mine.

I looked down at the crabs as they sidled around the bucket.

'So, how've you been?' he continued. 'You look great, you haven't changed a bit.'

'Well, I don't think that's true, but thank you.'

'Is this your daughter?'

I nodded. 'Lucy, say hi to Tadgh.'

'Hi-lo, Tadgh.'

'Pleased to meet you, Lucy,' he said, proffering his hand.

She scrunched up her nose in disgust at the hand that had just held a crab. 'Urgh, yacky hands.'

We started to laugh.

'I don't blame you,' Tadgh said to her before looking back at me. 'She looks just like you.'

I had always thought she looked more like Joe, but maybe Tadgh could see some of me in her.

'So, how've you been? Still living in Dublin?'

I nodded.

'Are you back visiting your folks?'

'Just for a few days. How's everything with you?'

'Well, I'm still running the restaurant and it's busy, thank God, especially now we're coming into the summer season. Would you believe that Senan will be doing his Leaving Cert next month and, all going well, will be heading to college in September?'

'Wow, that makes me feel old.'

'Tell me about it,' he said, laughing. 'I heard you married Joe de Paor,' he said after a pause. 'Your parents keep me up to date with all your comings and goings.'

I nodded, unable to find any words.

'I see his work mentioned in the papers from time to time. He seems to be doing really well.'

'What about you? Are you married?' I asked, keen to move the conversation away from Joe.

He looked momentarily wounded. 'No ... I guess I've been busy with the restaurant, and Senan, of course.'

Awkwardness charged the air between us. I found myself unable to say anything. It was as if my brain had abandoned me.

'Well, it's been really good to see you, Penny. I'd better take these guys back to the restaurant.' He indicated the bucket. 'I've a full house tonight. Why don't you and Lucy drop by for lunch some day? I'd love you to see it – it's changed a lot since you were last there.'

'Sure, Tadgh, that would be lovely.'

But I knew as I said the words, I was just paying him lip service. I had avoided his restaurant ever since I had left Inishbeg Cove, and I certainly wouldn't be going there this time either.

E very day in the village seemed to last an eternity. Lucy woke early each morning and I took her down to the cove so she wouldn't wake Mam and Dad. We would run along the sand together or play with her bucket and spade underneath the indigo sky as the sun rose over the Atlantic. Then, as the sky transmuted to shades of blue, we would return to the house, where Mam and Dad would just be getting up, and we would all eat breakfast together. Somehow, we had slotted into this routine over the last few mornings.

I still hadn't heard from Joe. I decided that I would give him a week to get his head together and then – well, I wasn't sure what I would do. I was willing the days to pass until the interminable wait had ended. I hated being in this limbo state. I desperately wanted to talk to him, to know what was going on inside his head, but I had to give him space. He'd been under a lot of pressure lately. His last piece had failed to meet the reserve at auction, and there had been a scathing write-up afterwards in the Culture section of the

Sunday Times titled 'Joe de Paor – Creative Genius or Emperor's New Clothes?'. He claimed he never listened to the critics, but I could tell he was wounded. I knew how fragile an artist's ego could be – especially his. The review in the *Times* had really knocked him, and he had been moody and distant ever since.

Rogue thoughts infiltrated my mind as I lay awake at night: what if after a week he decided that he needed more time? What would I do then? But I pushed the worries out again as quickly as they entered. However he felt about me, he would surely need – and want – to see Lucy, wouldn't he? I willed the days to hurry past until it was Saturday – exactly a week since I had left.

It worried me how quickly Lucy had stopped asking about her father. She was in great form, and I was relieved to see she was oblivious to the worries that clouded my head. She was loving her stay in Inishbeg Cove and the attention being heaped on her by her doting grandparents. I marvelled at how happy and settled she had become there in just a few short days. She adored our morning trips to the beach or to Greg's ice-cream parlour. Sometimes Mam and Dad would bring her to the swings beside the village hall in the afternoon. It was as if she didn't notice Joe's absence at all. How I wished I could feel the same. I hated the unknown, I hated Mam delicately asking me whether everything was okay as she poured me another cup of tea, and having to lie to her and say yes, everything was fine. My parents were in their sixties: they had spent enough years worrying about me growing up. I was an adult now; they didn't need me to be a burden on them.

SOMEHOW, Saturday finally arrived. That morning, after Lucy and I had eaten breakfast, I went down to the bedroom and rang Joe. The breath snagged in my chest as I waited for him to answer.

I couldn't believe he had made no effort to contact me. He hadn't even texted to see how Lucy was doing. I had thought he would have had a change of heart by now. I had expected him to beg me to come home because he missed us after only a couple of days. Could he really switch off from his own flesh and blood so easily? Being apart from Lucy for more than a few hours made me anxious; I certainly couldn't go a day, let alone a week, without an update on how she was. But then, what did I know about being an artist? Maybe the ability to shut out all other distractions – even the people you loved – and focus on your art was how you summoned up the creativity you needed to make a masterpiece.

Finally, he answered. My stomach felt as though it was tumbling around inside a washing machine.

'So, how've you been?' I began. My heart was hammering so loudly inside my ribcage that I was sure he would hear it on the other end of the phone.

Was I imagining it, or did I hear a frustrated sigh down the line? I could imagine him frowning.

'Up and down,' he said after a long pause.

I felt a sinking feeling deep in the pit of my stomach; he wasn't in a good mood, and this didn't bode well for our conversation.

'Have you had time to think?'

There was silence on the other end, and I instinctively knew that whatever Joe was going to say next wasn't good news.

'I need more time. I think I'm all out. I feel the well is dried up.'

'But it's unfair on me and Lucy!' I protested. 'You've forced us out of our home, Joe.'

'You can come home any time, Penny. You don't have to make everything so dramatic. I can sleep at the studio.'

'Are you serious?'

'When will you ever begin to understand how all-encompassing this job is? It's not an office job where I clock in at nine and out again at five – it's in my head all day, every day. There's no escape from it!' His voice was agitated.

'Joe, I know your job isn't easy,' I reasoned, 'but it's not life or death if you don't paint. So what if you can't create anything for a few months? We've plenty of savings – we'll survive. I can even go out and get a job to help take some of the stress off you. Don't let the pressure get to you. Maybe what you need is to free your mind and then the creativity will come—'

'What the hell do you know about art, Penny?' he spat.

That stung. He was frustrated and angry, and he was using me as his punchbag. I know people say that we hurt the people we love the most, but I was sick of justifying his mood swings.

The thing with Joe was, I never knew which version of him I was going to get. His moods were so erratic. Some days I woke up to calm Joe and all was fine, but there were many days of distant Joe when he seemed so far out of reach, as if there was a glass partition between us. Of course he could be loving too; on those days he was kind and attentive and made me feel as though I was the only woman who understood him, as if I was essential to both his life and his art. That I was the only person on Earth who could complete him. When Joe was focused on me, it was the best place in the world to be. It was like sunshine warming my skin on a summer's day. But I was sick of walking on eggshells around him. I had feelings and needs too; Joe de Paor wasn't the only person in this marriage.

I took a deep breath, and the words I had wanted to say for a long time tumbled out: 'I might not know anything about art, but I do know about being a loving, caring wife, and I'm a damn good mother. I've always tried to under-stand your ways and give you everything you need to create, but I can't deal with any more of your moods, Joe. Take all the time you need. Lucy and I are staying in Inishbeg Cove!' Then I ended the call and stood stock still in my bedroom, in shock. I couldn't believe I had done that. Me. I had hung up on Joe.

'Who was that?' Mam asked, coming into the bedroom, her eyebrows raised. She had obviously been earwigging on our conversation.

'Joe.' I sighed, sitting down on the side of the bed, still in shock. Had I really just uttered those words? I had effec-tively told him I was leaving him. The whole thing felt surreal.

'Is everything okay, Penny?' She sat down beside me. 'You don't have to put on a brave face for me, y'know?' Her voice was soft and warm, like a blanket, and there was some-thing about her words and us sitting on the side of my child-hood bed that brought me back to being a little girl again. I remembered when I was five years old and Mam had comforted me after I had fallen off my bike, or when I was eight and had had had a fight with Michelle O'Dowd in school. She had comforted me in the same way, and I needed her just as much now as I had then.

'Come here, *a ghrá*,' she soothed as tears came spilling out of me. I couldn't stop them. Mam didn't ask any questions; she put her arm around me and stroked my hair so that I breathed in the floral notes of her perfume, mixed with her comforting smell.

'I think my marriage might be over, Mam,' I whispered.

8

SARAH

The day after the wedding, Greg and I went to see Dr Kerridge, who had recently taken over from old Dr Fitzmaurice, to have the pregnancy confirmed. Much to my surprise, he estimated that I was about ten weeks along and congratulated us both with an enthusiastic handshake. When I mentioned my concerns about my age, he reassured me that every pregnancy came with its own risks, no matter what age the mother was, and I shouldn't get too hung up on it.

'You're fit and in good health,' he said. 'I've seen plenty of women your age and even older who had uncomplicated pregnancies and perfectly healthy babies, and I've seen women half of your age with difficult pregnancies. If you take it easy, eat well and receive the right maternal care, there is every reason to be optimistic.'

Greg and I left his surgery feeling overjoyed, as if we were dancing on the colour-streaks of a rainbow the whole way home.

The next day Greg went into Ballymcconnell and arrived

home with a book on pregnancy and a tiny white baby-gro with a yellow duck pattern running along the trim.

'Sorry, I couldn't help it,' he added apologetically, as if he were afraid I would be cross with him.

I wrapped him in a hug. 'How could I be cross with you? I love you and I love that you're excited for our baby.'

He placed a kiss on my forehead. 'I never thought I would get this lucky – thank you, Sarah.'

Greg was thrilled about the prospect of fatherhood. Ever since he had found out, his face had shone as he went about daily life but, even though Dr Kerridge had done his best to calm my fears, I still couldn't shift my niggling worries about my age. I was deliberately staying away from the internet, I was too afraid of what I would find if I began googling.

'I'm scared, Greg,' I had said as we sat up in bed together one night.

'But why? You heard what Dr Kerridge said – don't get hung up on your age.'

'I know, but it all just feels ... well, too good to be true.' I sighed. 'What if we've used up our share of good luck? I thought meeting you was as good as it got for me, and I was happy with that. I'm terrified that something horrible is going to happen to snatch it all away from me again. If we were in a movie, this is where a plague of flesh-eating locusts would descend on the village.'

Greg laughed. 'There are no weighing scales for luck, Sarah. It's not like a pizza, where you share it out so that everyone gets a slice. Sometimes good things just happen.' He shrugged. 'Some folks get lucky in life and some folks get screwed over. We've been lucky.'

'But even if we're lucky and our baby is born healthy,' I went on, 'as older parents, will we have the energy to deal with a baby? You should see some of the bleary-eyed mammies that come into the post office after they've been up half the night with a teething baby or a sick toddler. Or what about having the stamina to run around and play football with them when they're a bit older? I'll be almost forty-two when the little one is born, which means I'll be forty-seven by the time they start primary school! The other parents at the school gate will probably think I'm the child's grandmother! Imagine, I'll be fifty-five by the time they're a teenager. They'll run rings around me!'

'Being in your forties today is different than it was in our parents' time,' Greg reassured her. 'People are healthier and live for longer. You need to stop focusing on our age and think of all the positive things we can give a baby, like love, stability, a comfortable home. Our baby will never want for anything, and there are a lot of parents half our age who can't offer that.'

Whenever I was feeling overwhelmed, Greg was able to calm me down and quiet the niggling voices in my head. He would patiently listen to my worries and was always there with an endless stream of reassurances.

And so, over the last few days I slowly allowed myself to accept the fact that this was really happening – that a baby was in our future. During quieter times in the post office I had let myself imagine what it would be like to be a mother and hold my baby in my arms. How it would feel to gently pull delicate arms through the sleeves of little knitted cardigans. To slide impossibly small scratch mittens over a tiny curled fist. And I couldn't think of a better place to raise a child than in our village. The fresh sea air, having the beach as your playground, the safety of knowing everyone – there was no better place to grow up.

My morning sickness seemed to have turned into 'all-day sickness' and from the moment I woke until I went to bed at night, I couldn't keep anything down. But Dr Kerridge had told me it was a sign that the pregnancy was progressing well, which was reassuring.

We were counting down the days to our first hospital appointment, when we would see our baby on a scan. We still hadn't told a soul; we had agreed to wait until after the twelve-week mark, when Dr Kerridge had told us the chances of miscarriage were markedly reduced. I was sure Mrs Manning had already guessed, though. She had remarked that I looked 'peaky' one day when she had come into the post office for a chat. I had tried to fob it off as tiredness after the wedding, but she had a knowing smile on her face. You couldn't keep a secret from Mrs Manning. I hoped that the scan would help me to relax a little. *If you make it that far,* the nagging voice in my head chimed in.

Someone was pulling at my eyelids. I opened my eyes and looked around the room. Bright sunlight crept around the edges of the blind. For a moment I was confused about where I was but then it hit me afresh, like it did every morning when I woke.

'Wake up, Mama,' Lucy demanded.

I pulled myself upright and leant back against the pillows. 'Hello, baby girl.'

'Get up, Mama, me wanna go to the beach!'

'I'll take you, Lucy,' Mam said, gently opening the bedroom door. 'We'll let your mammy sleep on, okay, love?'

Lucy bounced out of bed and ran into her grandmother's arms. I turned over and realised that the pillow was wet beneath my face. I had obviously been crying in my sleep again.

Over the last few days I had fallen into a fog of depression. Mam and Dad had stepped in to take care of Lucy, as I could barely climb out of bed. Joe hadn't called me, and I was starting to realise that things were really over between us. I felt bruised and embarrassed. I regretted the conversation we had had so much. Why hadn't I just taken Lucy back to Dublin and let Joe sleep in the studio if that was what he wanted? Surely that would have been better than the awful pain that seared my heart now. But then I thought of Lucy. I owed it to her not to live a life dictated by her father's whims.

I had given so much of my life to Joe, and now I was left with nothing. He had infiltrated my thoughts and opinions until I really didn't know myself any more. Then I thought of Lucy's pure smile and I knew that I had the best gift of all, but I was worried about the future.

One morning several days later, Lucy came bounding into the bedroom and jumped on top of me. Mam followed her, pulled back the curtains then opened the window, letting cool morning air rush into the room.

'It's a beautiful day out there,' she began. 'It's almost a sin to be in bed in this weather. Come on, up you get. I promised Lucy we'd bring her to Greg's for an ice cream.'

I groaned. I knew she meant well, but I didn't want to face anyone. I didn't want to have to make inane chit-chat with all the villagers we would inevitably meet on the short walk down the main street. They would ask about Joe and I didn't trust myself to be able to hold it together.

'You take her, Mam,' I pleaded, turning over in bed. 'I'm too tired.'

'Penny, you need to get up out of that bed this minute!' she said in a voice that reminded me of when she'd told me to get up for school as a teenager. 'I know you're going through a hard time,' she went on, 'but you're a mother – you have someone else to think of besides yourself, and Lucy needs her mammy right now. Come on, you can't disappoint her. I promised her an ice cream for being so good.'

I knew Mam was emotionally blackmailing me.

'Up, Mama, me wanna ice cream,' Lucy demanded, tugging my hand underneath the blankets.

I looked at her sweet round face and knew I couldn't disappoint her.

'All right then,' I said, pulling back the rose-printed duvet cover and putting my feet on the floor. 'Let's get ice cream.'

After I had showered and dressed, I made my way down to the kitchen.

'What will you have for breakfast?' Mam asked.

'I'm not hungry.'

'You're fading away, Penny, and God knows, you didn't have much weight on you to begin with. You need to look after yourself, or how will you ever mind Lucy?'

Once again, she had played the guilt card. Grudgingly I took a buttered slice of toast and forced myself to eat it, even though it tasted like cardboard in my mouth.

'Me going to get the biggest ice cream,' Lucy said, bouncing around on the chair beside me. She was grinning in pure excitement. I reached out and pulled her into a hug.

After I had eaten, we set off for the ice-cream parlour.

'How long has it been open?' I asked Mam as we arrived at the door. I noticed the wall outside was decorated with plaques from various awards his ice-cream had won.

'Greg opened it shortly after he moved into the village. He was an attorney over in America, would you believe?' She emphasised the word 'attorney'. 'He had a big job, but he gave it all up when he met Sarah.'

Lucky Sarah, I thought, feeling a pang of heartache.

'He was fed up of the rat-race and he had always dreamed about opening his own business and that's when he realised with tourist numbers growing in the village every year, there would be a market for an ice-cream parlour, and he wasn't wrong. He opened it late last year and it's been doing a bomb ever since,' Mam went on.

We pushed the door open and a bell tinkled to announce our arrival. The café was decorated in a retro American style, and an old-fashioned push-button till stood on the counter.

A group of teenagers were sitting on the tall stools at the curved counter. We sat in a booth and a man, who I presumed was Greg, came over with menus.

'Greg, I'd like you to meet my daughter Penny and my granddaughter Lucy,' Mam beamed.

'Pleased to meet you,' Greg said, offering me his hand. He was ruggedly handsome, with dark stubble dotting his jaw and clear blue eyes. Even the silly hat he was wearing, which sat at a jaunty angle, couldn't disguise his good looks. 'I've heard loads about you.'

I smiled awkwardly. 'All good, I hope.'

'Absolutely!' He grinned, showing off perfect American teeth.

'Are you and Sarah not heading off on a honeymoon?' Mam asked.

Greg shook his head and laughed. 'No, I couldn't persuade Sarah to leave the post office.'

'She works too hard,' Mam said.

Greg left us to peruse the menu. As I read, I saw that everything was made in-house.

'He gets the milk and cream from Galvin's farm out the road,' Mam said. 'Then he makes all his own ice cream and supplies it to a lot of the restaurants around the county.'

I was impressed. I had to admit, the café was very cool – the kind of place you might find in Dublin or Cork, not Inishbeg Cove.

When Greg returned, Mam ordered a brown bread and toffee twist ice cream. Even though I didn't feel like eating, I chose the Inishbeg Cove sea-salted caramel because I felt I should order something.

'Save the best until last. What can I get you, little lady?' Greg asked Lucy.

She pointed to the image of a unicorn ice cream on the children's menu.

'Great choice,' he said, taking our menus.

After a few minutes Greg returned with our ice creams. Mine arrived in a large sundae glass with warm caramel sauce on top. I felt queasy just looking at it. Lucy's was vanilla ice cream with a unicorn-shaped wafer sticking out of it, accompanied by three little bowls of toppings: chocolate buttons, pastel-coloured sprinkles and mini marshmallows. I didn't want to think about how much sugar was in it. Her face lit up with excitement as Greg placed her ice cream in front of her, and my heart swelled. Mam had been right. I couldn't stay in bed moping any more; it wasn't fair on Lucy. I dipped my spoon into the sauce and brought it to my lips. It was as smooth as silk. At any other time it would have been divine, but my appetite just wasn't up to it. I pushed the glass away.

Suddenly I spotted Tadgh at the counter, chatting to Greg. Greg disappeared for a few minutes then returned with three tubs of ice cream and handed them to Tadgh.

'Hey there,' Tadgh said, stopping at our table on the way out. He nodded at Mam. 'Hello, Mrs Murphy.'

'How are you, Tadgh?' Mam said, smiling.

'I thought you would have gone home?' he said, looking at me.

'I decided to stay on a bit longer.' I looked down at my fingers as they twirled the spoon through the sticky caramel.

'You never took me up on the offer of a free lunch. Please say you'll come.'

'Sure,' I said, deliberately non-committal.

'How about tomorrow?' he continued. 'Wednesday isn't usually too busy, so I'll be able to escape the kitchen and join you for a bit. I'll make sure I've something extra-special on the menu for Lucy.'

Lucy beamed up at him.

'They'd love to,' Mam cut in before I had a chance to think of an excuse.

I glared at her, but she and Tadgh were too busy smiling at one another to catch my annoyance. She'd always had a soft spot for him.

'Great,' I said, forcing myself to sound enthusiastic.

'He's a lovely fella,' Mam said after he had left. I knew she had never understood why we broke up.

I groaned internally. Having an awkward lunch with Tadgh was the last thing I needed.

10

'What are you doing lifting that?' Greg said as he came in the door of the post office. 'Give it here.' He rushed over and took the parcel from me. 'You should be taking it easy!'

'In case you haven't noticed, I work in a post office and lifting parcels is part and *parcel* of the job.' I laughed at my own pun.

'Very funny,' Greg said.

'Anyway, it's not that heavy.'

'Hmm.' He remained unconvinced. 'So, are you ready to go?'

'Almost. Just let me put a sign up on the door so the villagers know I'm closed for a few hours.'

The day had finally arrived for my first appointment at the maternity hospital. I had lost count of the number of times I had been sick that morning, and I was beginning to suspect that nerves were making my morning sickness worse.

'I'm so excited,' Greg said as we sat in the car. 'My head

is all over the place. I couldn't concentrate on anything in work.'

We seemed to have such different outlooks on this pregnancy, Greg was Pollyanna-ish in his eternal optimism, but I was more cautious. Realistic.

We set off for the hospital, but driving over the winding mountainous roads did nothing for my nausea. I had the window rolled down as Greg drove along, so fresh air could rush in. I looked out at the patchwork of green fields dotted with marigold-coloured furze under a slate-grey sky. The colours were so vivid, the hues so dramatic. I had driven over these same roads so many times since I was a child but, no matter how often I crossed them, the view down to the coast from the mountains never failed to take my breath away. Lots of people woke up to a view of concrete or grey skies as far as the eye could see – I felt so lucky to live on the very edge of Ireland. We saw the elements in all their technicolour glory every day. I hoped our child would grow up to appreciate it and be proud of being raised in the remote village, like I was. So many of the girls I'd gone to school with had found the village too small. They couldn't wait to leave and go to college, but I had never felt that pull. Inishbeg Cove was the only place I ever wanted to call home.

Just under two hours later, Greg turned the car into the hospital car park. I got out, stretched my legs and breathed the fresh air deeply into my lungs. I caught sight of a solitary magpie, eyeballing me from his perch on a nearby fence. A shiver spread through my body. *Not today*, I thought. I had always hated magpies. My mother had been really superstitious about them, and it had rubbed off on me. I saluted him to ward off any bad luck he might be sending my way, and we went into the hospital. As much as

I was excited, I was also petrified that something would go wrong.

We followed the signs to the antenatal area and took a seat in the waiting room, where we were eventually greeted by a brusque but smiling doctor. She showed us into her examining room.

'I'm Dr Hilary McCabe. I'll be the obstetrician overseeing your pregnancy. Climb up onto the bed there and let's take a look.'

I did as I was told, and lay back as Dr McCabe began to spread cool jelly across my abdomen and started to move the probe around. She remained silent for what felt like an age. Greg and I held our breath, neither of us daring to talk.

'Look, here is your baby,' Dr McCabe said eventually. She pointed at the screen, where we could see the blurry outline of a baby.

'So, the baby is okay?' Greg asked, nerves dancing in his voice.

'The baby is perfect.'

Relief and gratitude flooded through me. I said a silent 'thank you' to my parents in heaven. I knew they were looking down on me today.

'Oh, wait...' Dr McCabe said suddenly, studying the screen closely. Her face was screwed up as she stared at it intently.

My heart fell. Something was wrong. I knew it was too good to be true.

'What is it?' Greg asked quickly.

Dr McCabe didn't reply as she moved the probe around, sticking it even harder into my stomach.

'What's wrong?' I asked, tensing in panic.

Eventually the doctor spoke. 'Sarah, there's another baby in here.'

I couldn't comprehend what she was saying until Greg started to laugh. 'Twins? You mean we're actually having twins?'

'Congratulations!' Dr McCabe beamed. 'Look – the second baby is hiding behind this one, which is why I missed it on first glance.' She moved the probe. Although it was hard to see, I could make out the outline of two babies.

'Oh my God, Sarah, can you believe it?' Greg said, grinning at me. He stood up and moved closer to the screen to get a better look.

'Look, here's Twin 1 and over here is Twin 2, sucking their thumb.'

Greg and I watched in awe as our two babies kicked their little legs. A tear wound its way down my cheek. It was real – this was really happening. Greg gave my hand a squeeze.

'Now I need to do some measurements to make sure everything is as it should be.'

We watched as the doctor clicked and dragged lines across the screen. Our eyes were fixed on the monitor as we tried to make sense of the blur of black and white.

'Hmm,' the doctor said eventually. 'It seems to be a monochorionic, diamniotic pregnancy.' Her voice had taken on an edge of caution.

'A what?' Greg and I asked in unison.

'"Monochorionic diamniotic" is the clinical term we use for identical twins who each have their own sac but who share a placenta. Sometimes we see identical twins with their own placentas, but your babies share a placenta. I must warn you both, there are higher risks associated with this type of twin pregnancy.'

Alarm bells started to ring in my head. 'What kinds of risks?' I asked, feeling out of my depth.

'Although the fact that each baby is in its own sac is good news, as it lessens the risk of cord entanglement, there are still risks due to the shared placenta.'

It felt as though the doctor was throwing out dangers like a circus performer throws knives. Immediately I felt naïve. Just seconds ago, I'd been so excited to be told we were having two babies; I hadn't stopped to think about the extra risks a twin pregnancy could bring.

She continued. 'This type of pregnancy, coupled with the risks of being a geriatric mother—'

Geriatric! Had I heard her correctly?

'Excuse me?' Greg said, a touch of defensiveness in his tone.

'Oh, apologies.' She laughed and gave a breezy wave of her hand. 'I'm not meant to use that term anymore. It's a horrible term we in the medical profession use for any mother over the age of thirty-five. Nowadays we're being encouraged to use the phrase, 'advanced maternal age' although that's not much better...'

All the original doubts crowded back into my mind. Even though the doctor was being kind, she had reinforced my anxieties. In the eyes of the medical profession, I was over the hill. Having one baby at my age was sheer and utter madness, let alone having twins.

Dr McCabe went on. 'Sarah, you are forty-one years of age. Advanced maternal age brings its own risks, such as high blood pressure and pre-eclampsia. Then when you throw in the risks associated with a twin pregnancy, as well as issues specific to identical twins, such as twin-to-twin transfusion syndrome, then this is a high-risk pregnancy. We will be keeping an extra-close eye on you. We'll need to scan you every two weeks to see how the babies are doing.'

'I see,' I said, completely deflated. I didn't know whether

to celebrate the fact that we were having twins or worry about it. It seemed that as soon as I allowed myself to get excited, I was quickly pulled back down again.

A short while later Greg and I left Dr McCabe's office in stunned silence. Twins. We were having twins. Just when I thought I had maxed out on my good fortune to be pregnant at all, here I was getting not just one, but two babies. Although I was delighted, I was just as terrified. When I thought of the risks the doctor had mentioned, my stomach sank.

As we walked back out to the car park, my head was spinning with medical terms that an hour ago had meant nothing to me. All I could see around me were young women in their prime, blooming with health and radiance, not women like me, who stood in front of the mirror every morning plucking grey hairs from around their temple and watching in despair as their laughter lines got deeper by the day.

'I just can't believe it,' Greg gushed, shaking his head. 'It's such a shock. I have no family history of twins, as far as I know...'

He sounded ecstatic. He was already getting carried away and thinking about the future, but I was too afraid to let my head go there. I couldn't seem to jump on board Greg's train of optimism.

'I wonder if they'll be two boys or two girls?' he went on, chatting non-stop as we drove home along the coast road. 'If they're two girls, they'll rule the house. I'll be surrounded by women. Or if it's two little boys, they'll run riot. I always wanted a brother or sister when I was a kid – just think of all the fun they will have growing up. They will always have a best friend by their side.'

Greg and I were both only children. I was excited that

our babies would have a companion from the moment they were born.

'Well, maybe we shouldn't get too excited yet,' I cautioned, turning to look at Greg. 'You heard all the risks the doctor mentioned.'

'Don't worry about that right now,' Greg advised. 'We were given these babies for a reason. Let's take it one day at a time. We'll get through whatever is thrown at us. Let's focus on the fact that you have two babies growing in there, and I'm going to help you do everything we can to get them here safely.'

I knew he was right, but I still couldn't shake off my worry that this was too good to be true. The nagging doubts at the back of my mind that had started as whispers had grown louder; something was going to go wrong.

'Y ou wake, Mama?'

'I am now,' I said.

Lucy pulled my arm. 'It's morning time,' she sang. 'Let's get up.'

With Mam's words from the day before still ringing in my ears, I knew I couldn't stay moping in bed like I had for the last few mornings. Instead, I pulled back the duvet, swung my feet onto the floor and got up. Mam was right – Lucy deserved better. I owed it to my daughter to be functional, even if all I wanted to do was to fall asleep and never wake up again.

I wrapped Lucy in her dressing gown so that she looked like a squidgy marshmallow, then we headed down to the kitchen, where Mam was cleaning the window.

'Would you look at the dirt on that glass?' she said as we came into the room. Slanted beams of sunlight shone into the kitchen and dust motes danced in the warm rays. Lucy ran over and hugged her grandmother straight away while I sat down at the kitchen table.

'How's my best girl?' Mam said, lifting Lucy up. In the

few weeks we had been here, an undeniably close bond had been forged between them. It was going to be very difficult for everyone when the time came for Lucy and me to go home.

'Did you sleep okay?' Mam asked.

'Yes,' I lied. She didn't need to know that I had spent the night tossing and turning, overthinking everything Joe had ever said to me.

'So, are you going to Tadgh's today?'

'Well, I'm not s—'

'You're going!' Mam said, cutting across me.

'I'm not eight years old, Mam. You can't tell me who to play with.' Ever since I had come back to stay, it was as if we had reverted to our mother–child roles. It annoyed me that Mam had forgotten that I was a fully grown woman, capable of making my own decisions.

She inhaled sharply and I knew that I was in for a tirade.

'Penny,' she began, 'Tadgh has invited you to his restaurant – a restaurant that has won *numerous* awards and is held in *very* high esteem. I didn't raise you to be so rude. It must be all that time you've spent in Dublin!' She said 'Dublin' as if it was located on the far side of the moon.

'Well, if it means that much to you, I'll go then!' I snapped.

'Great.' She smacked her lips together with satisfaction, paying no attention to my petulant tone. 'And make sure you don't wear that tracksuit you've been living in for the last week. You'll feel much better if you put on a nice dress, and a bit of make-up wouldn't go amiss...'

I groaned internally, then pushed back my chair and got up to begin making breakfast for everyone.

Later, as I stood in the shower washing my hair, I replayed our conversation. How dare Mam tell me what to wear! My marriage was on the rocks – so what if I had worn a tracksuit for the last week? That was the least of my worries. I wasn't a child any more; I was capable of choosing my own clothes. This house wasn't big enough for the two of us. I needed to decide what Lucy and I were going to do, and where we were going to live, before I said something I would regret.

When I returned to the kitchen, I saw that Mam had dressed Lucy in a pretty blue-and-white striped sundress. She had managed to tame her curls and had put pink clips in her hair to keep it back off her face. Although Lucy looked adorable, it irritated me that Mam was clearly pulling out all the stops for Tadgh.

'You yook nice, Mama,' Lucy said. Despite Mam's fashion advice, I had decided to wear jeans and a simple, primrose-yellow blouse.

'Thank you, Lucy Lu. So do you.'

'There,' Mam said, standing back to admire us both. 'Aren't you a fine pair? Now, you'd better get going. You don't want to keep Tadgh waiting.'

'Heaven forbid...' I muttered.

Lucy and I set off along the cliff path. The path climbed higher until the sea twinkled silver beneath us, a rickety rail being the only thing separating us from a perilous drop. How many times had I walked along this path to visit Tadgh in the restaurant as a teenager? I wondered.

Soon we reached the cliff face into which the restaurant was set into a natural cavern in the stone. I tried to work out how long it had been since I was last there. It had probably been just after Tadgh's parents had died. During that time, he had worked manically, trying his best to keep the business afloat in the haze of his grief.

I pushed the door and entered under the stone archway that led into the restaurant. As I looked around, I saw that a lot had changed since the last time I was there. I was surprised to see that the restaurant had a stylish modern interior that went well with the raw stone of the walls. Candlelight flickered softly off the walls, giving the space an intimate feel. There were a couple of other diners, but I didn't recognise them as being from the village. I saw Tadgh standing behind the reception desk.

'Ah, you came!' he said, coming out to greet us. 'Will we sit over here?' He gestured to a nearby table.

'Sure,' I said, following him.

'Would Lucy like to colour, or I can get a jigsaw... I have a few little games to keep young diners occupied.'

'Some colouring would be perfect, thanks.'

He vanished behind the reception desk again and returned a minute later with a container of stubby crayons and a colouring book.

Lucy immediately set to work, leaving an awkward silence.

'Oh sorry, I should have given you a menu.' He jumped up once more and returned a moment later with a leather-bound menu, which he handed to me.

'So, what do you think you'll order?' he asked after a few minutes.

'Well, what does the chef recommend?'

'The line-caught sea bream is good – literally just off the boat this morning.'

'Great, I'll go with that.'

'I've made homemade fish bites for Lucy – there's no salt or anything in them. I hope she'll eat them.'

'Sounds perfect,' I said, closing the menu.

'Let me just tell them in the kitchen.'

He came back a couple of minutes later and sat back down.

'The restaurant looks great,' I said. 'You've done a lot of work on it.'

'It needed an overhaul. For years after Mam and Dad passed away, I guess it became like a shrine to them. I was afraid to change anything in case I was betraying their memory, but business was slowing down. One day I realised I could either keep going as I was and watch the business go under or I could try to put my own stamp on things, so that's what I did. Thank God, it's gone from strength to strength ever since. I have two chefs helping me out during the summer season, I have six waiting staff, and Senan gives me a hand when he's not in school or studying.'

Tadgh's words reminded me of that awful time in his life. He'd been so young when all that responsibility had landed squarely upon him. Tadgh had been orphaned when his parents were killed by a drunk driver on their way home from a day of Christmas shopping in Limerick. Tadgh and Senan had been in the back seat and had miraculously survived with minor injuries. He had only been eighteen and Senan six. Suddenly Tadgh had been catapulted from being a carefree teenager into parenting his younger brother and trying to keep the family business afloat. Tadgh and I had been a couple for two years at that stage – an eternity for a teenage romance. We had planned on going to college together in Dublin once we'd finished school, but everything changed between us when his parents died. We went from seeing each other every day to barely seeing one another because he was busy working in the restaurant – or, if he wasn't working, he was taking care of Senan. Tadgh changed overnight; he suddenly grew serious and more mature, and no longer laughed at the things we had once thought were funny. I would call into the restaurant to see him, but he would be under pressure in the kitchen and I knew I was getting in the way. I felt like I was last on his list, but I understood that it wasn't his fault. If anything, I admired how he had risen to the challenges life had thrown at him, but we were too young for our relationship to survive such a massive change.

One day, just before my Leaving Cert exams, things came to a head between us, and I told him that perhaps we should take a break for a while. I hadn't expected Tadgh to agree with me. I had hoped my words might wake him up and make him realise how dangerously close to the brink our relationship was teetering, but he had said that I was right. As we had sat on the wall of the cove, kicking our heels against the stone, looking out on the horizon, I will never forget the wounded expression on his face. His eyes, which were still heavy with the pain of losing his parents, took on a haunted look. Then he had stood up and as tears ran down my face, my boyfriend walked away from me for the last time.

A few months later, it was time for me to go to college in Dublin. I was heartbroken to leave the village alone. Tadgh and I should have been heading off together; it should have been an exciting new adventure for both of us, but it wasn't to be. Although initially I had missed Tadgh dearly, gradually I became immersed in city life and felt my wounded heart start to heal. As deadlines for assignments and exams loomed, I began coming home less at the weekends, choosing to spend them in Dublin instead. It was also around this time that I met Joe. Although he was much older than I was, there was an undeniable spark between us. He was an enigma, like nobody I had ever met before. He didn't hide behind his feelings; he made it perfectly obvious from the day we met that he liked me, that he *needed* me, whereas in my relationship with Tadgh I had felt I was last on the long list of his priorities.

I had deliberately avoided the restaurant on my visits home over the years so, since the day we broke up, I hadn't set eyes on Tadgh until the day we met on the beach. Of course, Mam and Dad kept me up to date on his comings and goings. They always sounded wistful whenever they mentioned his name, and I knew they wondered why I hadn't chosen someone solid like Tadgh to settle down with instead of the unpredictable Joe.

'So, how's life in Dublin?' Tadgh asked bringing me out of my thoughts as he poured me a glass of chilled white wine.

'Great,' I lied.

'And Joe, is he busy?'

'Yes, he's getting ready for his next exhibition.' I traced my finger along the slender stem of the glass.

'Wow, it must be amazing to see work you create being displayed in a gallery. What a feeling.'

'I guess so...' I shifted in my chair. I didn't want to talk about Joe, especially not to Tadgh.

'So how much longer do you think you will be here?' he continued.

I picked up a crayon and began helping Lucy to colour a flower. 'I'm not sure, maybe another week or two...'

That was the question I had recently been asking myself: how much longer *was* I going to stay? One week had morphed into two, two had quickly moved into three. When would I be able to go back to my home in Dublin? Would I ever? Although I loved my parents dearly and appreciated them helping me out, I couldn't stay under their roof for the long term – Mam and I would murder one another. Plus, I needed my stuff. I had only taken a small case of clothes for Lucy and a few of her toys, but there were loads of things I had forgotten. I was putting off returning to Dublin because, when I did, I was terrified that it would be the end of everything. Taking my things would mean I'd surrendered. The final act in our marriage.

'He must be missing her,' Tadgh probed, jerking his head in Lucy's direction.

'Op, Mama,' Lucy cried, pushing my hand away from where I was colouring alongside her.

'She's bossy,' I said, deliberately avoiding his question. Was he just being nosy, I wondered, or did he suspect that there was something wrong between Joe and me?

'She reminds me of someone,' Tadgh said playfully.

Our food arrived, and I tucked into the seasoned sea bream served with baby potatoes and asparagus. The food was fresh, wholesome and simply presented. There were no fancy accompaniments or garnishes. I was genuinely impressed. Joe had an obsession with being seen in the latest eateries. If they had won an award, he would want to visit, but I could see that Tadgh's style was to let the food do the talking.

'This is so good, Tadgh. You'll have the Michelin guide out here soon.'

'They came a couple of years ago, actually, but I was furious.'

'Why on earth would you turn down such a prestigious award?' I was flummoxed.

'Ah, you know I hate all that pretentious nonsense,' he said, shaking his head. 'I don't want people to come here because they read about it in a guide and think they *should* eat here. I want people to come by word of mouth, on the recommendation of a friend.'

I could see the passion in his eyes as he talked about his food, and I loved how animated he had become.

'This is yummy,' Lucy said, smacking her lips as she devoured another fish bite.

'So, did you meet anyone else?' I dared to ask, turning the tables on him, feeling emboldened by the wine.

'After you, you mean?' he said, a glint in his eye. I studied the table linen for a moment before looking back up at him again. He shook his head. 'I was seeing a French girl for a few years – she worked here as a waitress, but it didn't work out between us.' He looked mournful, and I felt an unexpected twinge of jealousy for this girl, who he clearly had strong feelings for.

We chatted some more until Tadgh saw that his waiters were overstretched as more diners entered the restaurant. 'I'd better give them a hand,' he said, getting up to help clear off some tables.

'I should probably bring Lucy home anyway,' I said. Lucy was beginning to look restless, and I knew I was on borrowed time.

'Would you like to go for a drink one night? The Anchor has a *céilí* every Friday. It's always a good laugh.'

I couldn't believe *céilí* night still happened. I felt as if I had stepped back in time. When I was a child, Mam and Dad would get dressed up in their best clothes and head off to the *céilí*, leaving me to be looked after by my grandparents. They lived for the night but that had been nearly thirty years ago – had nothing changed since then? My face must have shown my surprise because he added, 'Just for old times' sake, before you go back to Dublin?'

Did he mean a drink or a *drink* drink?

'Well, I can't with Lucy...' I began, although I knew Mam

and Dad would have no problem babysitting her, especially if I was meeting Tadgh.

He shrugged. 'No worries. Maybe another time.'

'Yeah, maybe,' I said, then we said an awkward goodbye to one another.

As Lucy and I walked back home along the cliff path, she swung out of my hand, singing 'Ten Green Bottles' at the top of her voice. Despite my earlier reservations, I had to admit I had enjoyed the afternoon. The time had flown past, and it hadn't been as awkward as I had feared, but Tadgh's suggestion that we should go for a drink had caught me off guard. Maybe I was just overthinking things, but he had unsettled me. There was too much water under the bridge for us. Did he mean a friendly drink to catch up on old times, or was it something more? Or, maybe I was reading too much into it... Anyway, I told myself, either way it would be pointless to meet him because I wouldn't be staying in the village for much longer.

12

SARAH

One Sunday afternoon, Mrs Manning, Greg and I were sitting around the table in the cottage. Greg had made dinner and we had invited Mrs Manning to join us. We had eaten our fill of tender beef and crispy potatoes roasted in goose fat. As Mrs Manning filled us in on her week, I made to get up to clear the plates before we tucked into the rhubarb crumble I had made for dessert.

'Sit down – don't move,' Greg ordered, standing up instantly.

'Honestly, Greg,' I said, shaking my head. 'I'm only clearing a few plates!'

Mrs Manning raised her brows, looking at me, then at Greg, and finally back to me. 'Have you two got something you want to tell me?'

I turned to Greg and he nodded. We had passed the magical three-month mark – the stage where the books say that the risk of miscarriage is markedly reduced but I was still terrified to tell people. Once one person knew, the whole village would know within hours, and I was still anxious that things might not go smoothly.

'I'm pregnant, Mrs Manning,' I admitted.

'Oh, Sarah, that is wonderful, wonderful news!' she cried. She tried to get up from her chair to hug me.

'Don't get up!' I ordered. Instead I went over to the older lady and hugged her tightly.

'I guess that explains the tummy,' she said, nodding at my abdomen. 'I thought you were letting yourself go. I was thinking that married life was suiting you a bit too well!'

I placed my hands on my rapidly expanding abdomen and laughed. 'You wouldn't want to be sensitive around here!' I said, pretending to be offended.

'There's more...' Greg went on, his face aglow.

'What is it?' Mrs Manning looked as us expectantly.

'We're having twins!' Greg beamed, looking like the cat who had got the cream.

'My word, what good news that is – you are to be doubly blessed! This is the best news I've heard since 1976, when I found out that the woman my ex-husband left me for had left him!'

We all laughed.

'They're identical,' Greg continued. 'So we're either having two little boys or two little girls.'

'Oh, whatever they are, they'll be double trouble, I've no doubt. This is fantastic! I'll get everyone at mass to pray for you, even though I don't believe in all that stuff. Don't tell Father Byrne, but I just go along for the cup of tea afterwards,' she said with a theatrical wave of her hand.

'Well, we'll take all the prayers we can get,' I said, laughing at her.

As I had expected, our news spread like wildfire throughout the village and Mrs Manning wasn't the only one to be overjoyed by our news. Maureen – Greg's maternal aunt – hugged us, tears in her eyes, when we called over to Cove View to tell her the news. Since Greg had moved to the village, he and Maureen had grown close. She would reminisce fondly about her sister Della, and I knew Greg loved discovering more about his birth mother, who he had never known.

When I went to work the morning after our announcement, I had a queue of people lining up to congratulate me. It seemed as though the whole village was overjoyed by our news. Everyone was excited to see new blood being brought into the village. It was a sad fact that few babies were born in Inishbeg Cove these days, and so, the villagers were taking good care of me. They would rush to assist me if they saw me trying to lift a heavy parcel. Ruairí had taken to dropping me in a decaf coffee and a scone in the mornings. Even Ida the herbalist had come in with a strange seaweed concoction that she said would help with morning sickness, after I had dashed off to be sick one day when she had been in the queue, but it smelled abhorrent and I hadn't been able to stomach it so far.

I was still really struggling with the sickness. I thought it would have abated now that I was in my second trimester, but Mrs Manning had told me that she had been sick the whole way through her pregnancies. I hoped I wasn't going to be the same. I knew the fact that I was carrying twins meant everything was going to be heightened.

A few days later I was in the post office sorting through letters when I felt that familiar heat break out all over my body and my mouth began to water. Beads of sweat prickled along the back of my neck and I knew I was going to be sick. Again. The post office door opened and Maureen came in.

'I'm going to be sick—' I blurted out before running out to the toilet, leaving her standing looking after me.

'Are you okay?' she asked when I returned a few minutes later. Although my stomach felt more settled now, after heaving up its contents into the toilet, things could change quickly. The waves of nausea never let up.

'I'll be fine,' I said. 'I just have to ride it out.'

'Well, they say that morning sickness is a good sign.'

'That's what Greg keeps saying.'

'I just wanted to drop these off for you. I've been knitting again – I can't seem to stop myself.' She laughed nervously.

Since we had announced our news, Maureen had been on a knitathon. She had already knitted mittens, socks and bonnets for both babies, and I knew she was working on blankets and teddy bears too.

Maureen and her husband Jim had met later in life, after the opportunity to have children of their own had passed them by, and she looked upon Greg as the son she'd never had. As soon as we had told her I was pregnant, she had slotted into an almost grandmotherly role, a role that Greg and I were only too happy to give her, because we knew we would need all the help we could get once the babies arrived. Our babies represented a chance for her to be involved in not just one, but two, infants' lives, and I could tell she was relishing the opportunity. She was already a huge support to us, and I knew she would be a great help when our babies arrived.

She handed me a paper bag. I opened it and lifted out two identical buttermilk-coloured cardigans, made from the softest wool.

'These are so beautiful.' I held them up to admire. 'Thank you, Maureen.'

It seemed that the whole of Inishbeg Cove was just as excited as Greg and I were about our twins. It was lovely to know that we had so many people in our corner wishing us well, but with that came a strange sense of pressure. I just hoped nothing would go wrong. I didn't want to let everyone down.

13

June arrived like a song of blue skies and warm sunshine. The summer season was now in full swing in Inishbeg Cove and, much to my dismay, I was still in the village. There was a new energy around the place, which always arrived with the tourists. Families picnicked in the cove while children swam in the sea. The shops were busier too, and it was hard to get a table in Ruairí's café and Greg's ice-cream parlour. When I was a child, Inishbeg Cove's location off the beaten track meant we only had a handful of tourists compared to what other seaside towns experienced, but in recent years, as word spread about the village's charms, it had been getting busier every summer.

All around me were signs that time was passing, and I had to decide what Lucy and I were going to do. Although Joe had called a few times, it had only been to ask about Lucy. He had made no reference to our marriage or said that he was missing us. As the days went by, I was becoming less optimistic of things working out between us.

Lucy and I couldn't live with my parents forever.

Although I appreciated them taking us in and all their help, Mam and I would come to blows soon if I didn't move out. She seemed to have forgotten that I was an adult, and I found myself having to bite my tongue. A lot. I had thought about taking Lucy back to Dublin. I could rent an apartment. It would give Joe space to get his head together and allow Lucy and me to pick up some semblance of our old life. But before I could do that, I had to find a job to support us – and that would mean arranging childcare for Lucy first. All the decisions that had to be made overwhelmed me, and I was crippled by my inability to plan for our future – a future that, if my worst fears came true, might be without Joe.

One afternoon I was sitting in the kitchen with a cup of tea when Mam arrived home from the playground with Lucy.

'Ook, what I got, Mama!' she said popping a lollipop out from her mouth and showing it off proudly. 'Ganny got me lots of sweeties.'

'Oh, did she now?' I said, raising my brows at my mother.

'So what if I did?' Mam challenged me. 'If a grandmother can't give her grandchild a few sweets, there's something wrong with the world!'

Even though I'd asked her not to, Mam constantly gave Lucy sweets, claiming it was 'a grandmother's prerogative'.

'Did you get me one?' I asked.

She shook her head. 'You're too big.'

I stuck my tongue out at her and she laughed. I pulled her onto my knee and let her head rest in the curve of my neck. Mam began unpacking the small bag of groceries she had got in O'Herlihy's.

'Not a bad day out there. The rain held off anyway.'

'Uh huh,' I said, not really paying attention.

'Did you hear the news?' she asked.

'No?'

'Sarah's pregnant.'

'They didn't hang around,' I said. 'Was it a shotgun wedding?'

'Stop that! We'll have none of that talk in this house,' Mam said, looking horrified. 'Anyway, we're all a lot more open-minded here nowadays.' She stopped for a breath. 'Would you believe it, they're having twins!'

'Wow, double trouble!'

'Well, I think it's a blessing. Sure, Sarah has the energy of a young one and Greg is very hands-on. They'll be fine.'

She walked over to put a litre of milk in the fridge.

'Ruairí needs a hand in the café,' she said over her shoulder as she closed the fridge door.

'And?' I asked, wondering why this news was relevant to me.

'Well, I told him you might be able to spare him a couple of hours—'

'You did *what*?'

'It's only for two hours a day, from twelve to two, to cover the lunchtime rush. Sure, we can mind Lucy for you—'

'I can't believe you did that, Mam! Why didn't you check with me first?'

She busied herself around the kitchen, her back to me. 'Sure, what else are you doing? It'll do you good to get out and about. Sitting in this kitchen staring at the same four walls, day in, day out, isn't going to help you.'

It irked me that everyone else seemed to think they knew what was best for me.

'But I'll be going back to Dublin soon!' I protested.

'Will you?' She turned around and looked steadily at me.

'Of course I will,' I said, trying to sound sure of myself but failing miserably.

'Look, pet,' she said kindly. 'I'm not having a go at you ... but do you think it might be time to accept that your marriage is over?'

I felt my bravado start to wobble in the face of her softness.

'Surely, Joe would have come down here by now if he was missing ye?' she continued. 'And I can't for the life of me understand how he can let that little girl go without giving her a second thought.' She shook her head.

That stung. She could say whatever she liked about Joe's feelings for me, but it hurt when she insinuated that he didn't care for our daughter.

'For your information, Joe has been phoning to chat to Lucy. Of course he cares about his child. But he isn't like everyone else; he's going through a really hard time. When he's caught up in his work, he can be ... well ... really intense. I know him. He just needs some time and space to get himself together and we'll be okay. I'm sure of it.' Why did I always feel the need to defend him? She had hit a nerve – I had asked myself the same questions. I blinked quickly to stop the tears from falling.

She came over to the table, placed her hand over mine and gave it a squeeze. 'We love you, Penny,' she said. 'We just want you to be happy.'

Instantly I felt guilty for snapping at her. To my parents, I was still their little girl. I knew I would feel the same if Lucy were in my shoes in the future. My parents just wanted to protect me from more heartbreak, but I was an adult and I had to live my own life, even if it ended in pain.

THE NEXT DAY, much to my disbelief, I found myself standing in Ruairí's kitchen hanging a striped apron around my neck. He had waved cheerily as I entered the café, clearly expecting me. I was fuming as I realised that Mam had obviously told him I would do the job without checking with me first.

I didn't know Ruairí well; he wasn't from the village. He was what the older people referred to as a 'blow in'. He had a frizzy ginger beard and a mass of red hair that he tried to tame into a bun.

He quickly explained how to use the sandwich maker, what the different settings on the coffee machine meant, and how I should grind the beans. He talked me through the menu and how to make the various sandwiches, wraps and panini until my head was spinning. Then he handed me a cloth and bottle of antibacterial spray and asked me to start by clearing some tables. As I went from table to table clearing disgusting, dirty plates and lipstick-stained mugs, I couldn't help wondering how I had ended up wiping down tables in the café in Inishbeg Cove. If you had told me a month ago that I would be doing this, I would have laughed in your face – but in just a few weeks my life had become unrecognisable to me. I had received a few texts from friends of mine in Dublin checking in to see if I was okay and I had lied and said I was having a lovely time spending the summer with my parents. I couldn't even begin to tell them the truth about my life; I knew they would never believe the transformation either.

'Make sure you use the spray, Penny,' Ruairí called to me, disturbing my thoughts. I grimaced a smile back at him and made an exaggerated show of spraying the table I was in the middle of cleaning.

The place was busy. There was a constant stream of

people sipping coffee or friends meeting over tea and scones, and the café buzzed with the hum of their chatter. The sea swimmers were warming up over coffee. I cringed as a few people I recognised came in. There were people I'd gone to school with, friends of my parents, and other familiar faces. I was sure they were wondering why I was working in the café when I was supposed to be married to a hotshot artist in Dublin.

I didn't have much time to dwell on it, as just then the lunchtime rush descended on the café. I was thrown in at the deep end: Ruairí put me in charge of the coffee machine while he made the sandwiches. I tried to remember the instructions for the different types of coffee, but I kept pressing the wrong buttons, causing the machine to hiss and splutter in protest. Ruairí was watching me over his shoulder, which just added to the pressure.

'Double trouble!' Ruairí shouted out behind me, and for a split second I wondered if it was another type of coffee that I was meant to know. I turned around to see he was talking to Sarah and Greg.

'Congratulations,' he continued.

'News travels fast.' They smiled adoringly at one another. They looked to be over the moon.

They ordered food then sat down at a table, chatting easily with one another. I couldn't help watching them. There was something simple, wholesome, about their love. Heaviness filled my heart. I couldn't imagine there was ever any drama in their relationship. Had Joe and I ever gazed so tenderly at each other? I realised with sudden clarity what it was about their relationship that intrigued me so much: it actually looked easy.

But I had no more time to analyse Sarah and Greg's relationship as Ruairí barked coffee order after coffee order to me. As I frothed milk for lattes and ground beans for Americanos, I barely got a chance to look up, let alone draw breath, and when he told me that it was after two o'clock and my first shift was finished, I was shocked. Despite my initial misgivings, I had to admit that the two hours had flown past.

'Thanks a million for today – you really dug me out of a hole,' Ruairí said as I removed my apron and hung it up on the back of the kitchen door.

'Don't mention it,' I said, slinging my handbag over my shoulder and heading for the door.

'See you at the same time tomorrow?'

I stopped and turned around. 'I don't know if Mam told you, but I might not be here for much longer.' It was only fair to let him know now so he couldn't accuse me of leaving him in the lurch when I went back to Dublin.

'Well, even if it's just for a few days, I'm glad of the extra pair of hands,' Ruairí said with a kind smile, his hazel eyes twinkling. 'See you tomorrow, Penny.'

14

PENNY

Since I had begun working in the café, the days had started to pass much faster. I was slowly starting to accept that maybe Mam had been right, and things were over between Joe and me. He called every few days to talk to Lucy, but nothing had changed. He still sounded frustrated and edgy, and I found my shoulders tensing up from just being on the other end of the phone to him. Although Lucy and I were very short on clothes, I still hadn't made the trip back to Dublin. I couldn't seem to summon the strength to do it. My biggest fear was that Joe wouldn't try to stop me if I left our Dublin home for good, and I still wasn't ready to say a final goodbye to him. So, for now, I was content to stay as I was. It pained me to look too far ahead. I couldn't think about what my life might look like without him in it. I had so many questions about the future – where would Lucy and I live? Would he try to fight me for custody? I could survive losing him, but I would never survive without Lucy. Some days, thinking about all the changes was so terrifying that I would feel my chest tighten and my heart start to thump. An angry buzzing would sound in my ears until I thought I might faint. Thinking too far into the future made me feel overwhelmed, so I tried to take things day by day. Then I broke each day down into manageable chunks and, somehow, I got through it that way. I got up in the mornings, brought Lucy for our daily run along the sand. Then we would return home for breakfast with Mam and Dad. Soon after that it would be time to go to the café for my shift. The only thing that gave me solace was that Lucy was happy and blissfully unaware of the turmoil in my heart. Mam and Dad were spoiling her, and she happily waved me off to work every day, knowing her grandparents would have a treat in store for her.

Much to my surprise, I found that I was actually enjoying working in the café. When I had started working there, as soon as the clock struck two o'clock, I would hurry to the cloakroom and throw my handbag over my shoulder, ready to go home, but now I looked forward to each shift. The café was usually so busy that the time flew past, and I didn't have a second to think about Joe. It was the only part of the day where he didn't infiltrate my thoughts and the minutes didn't drag.

Ruairí and I worked well together. I liked chatting with him as we frothed milk for lattes or buttered his famous Guinness bread. Sometimes, when it was really busy, I would stay on for another hour to help him out until it eventually quietened down. It gave me a sense of purpose and I was usually exhausted by the time I hung up my apron in the kitchen and said goodbye to him.

'Here, take home this tarte Tatin for your mam and dad, and bring home a slice of that rainbow cake for Lucy,' he would say. On other days it was a jar of his homemade jam or a few of his lemon curd buns. He always sent me home with something nice. Mam would put the kettle on as soon

as I came in and we'd all sit down at the table, eating
Ruairí's delicious treats with a cup of tea. It was a strangely
comforting routine – a routine that I probably would have
seen as pitiful a few weeks ago, but now it was one of the
highlights of my day.

'Penny?' Tadgh said, coming through the door one day
after the lunchtime rush had calmed down. 'I thought you'd
gone back to Dublin.'

'Nope, I'm still here,' I said with a grimace.

'If I'd known you were looking for a job, I could have
given you something in the restaurant,' he went on, looking
unperturbed by my sarcastic tone.

'I wasn't – well, not really. I'm just helping out on an ad
hoc basis,' I added, wincing. Why did I sound so formal?

'Oh, I see. We never got to have that drink—'

'Sorry, I've been really busy...' I began to rearrange the
jars of chutney that Ruairí had for sale on the counter.

'Well, how about tonight? It's *céilí* night.'

'I can't. I'm sure Mam and Dad will want to go to it.' I
knew they didn't go to it as frequently as they used to, but it
was a good excuse.

'What about tomorrow night? That will be quieter – give
us more of a chance to catch up.'

He wasn't giving up. I knew if I made another excuse, he
would just keep suggesting a different night.

I sighed internally. 'Sure.'

'Super. Is eight is okay with you?'

'Great,' I lied through gritted teeth.

'What's going on there?' Ruairí asked after Tadgh had
left.

'Oh, nothing.' I waved my hand. 'Tadgh and I used to go
out together years ago. It's just a bit awkward now being
back in the village...'

'You and Tadgh?' he said, nodding thoughtfully. 'Hmm.'

'What?'

'Don't tell him, but I've always had a thing for him. His brooding good looks and all that moody angst in his eyes ... aaah.' He sighed dramatically. 'Pity he's as straight as a pin.'

'You're gay?' I said.

'Pick up your jaw there, Penny,' he said. 'Didn't you know?'

I shook my head.

'God, I thought it was Inishbeg Cove's worst kept secret.'

'Are you in a relationship?' I asked.

He shook his head sadly. 'There isn't a lot to choose from in Inishbeg Cove – I think I am literally the only gay in the village. People who are gay usually head straight for the bright lights of Dublin or Cork. I was in a relationship with a chef who worked in Tadgh's for a while, but he moved on. He found the village too small. I've been single for three years now.'

'I can imagine it's slim pickings in a place like this.'

'So why the hell did you break up with the dreamy Tadgh?' He folded his arms across his chest, giving me his full attention.

'Oh, you know,' I said. 'Stupid teenage stuff. We were young.'

'Hmm ... something tells me there's more to that. Anyway, any word from you-know-who?'

He meant Joe. I had told Ruairí snippets of what had happened between us. He had listened, enthralled, before declaring that I was too good to be at Joe's beck and call. And even though he was saying the same things that Mam always said to me, somehow it didn't seem as harsh or judgemental when it came from Ruairí.

I shook my head, not trusting myself to speak.

'He doesn't deserve you, Penny. Dublin's loss is our gain!'
He pulled me into a hug. He smelled great, of citrus and
musk, and I found myself buoyed up by the compliment. I
realised how low my confidence really was. I had lived for so
long in Joe's shadow, waiting for him to throw crumbs of
affection my way. People were forever fussing and tiptoeing
around him, including me. Where had I gone to in that
time? The girl who had left Inishbeg Cove at eighteen?
Where was that girl – and her hopes, dreams and aspira-
tions? Deep down, all I wanted was for Joe to love me like I
had loved him, nothing more. I didn't want the prestige or
the fame of being married to Joe de Paor. I just wanted a
normal, loving relationship, like other people had. People
like Mam and Dad and, as I had seen over the last few
weeks, Sarah and Greg.

'It might not seem like it now, but you'll be okay,' he
reassured me.

My head knew that Ruairí was right, but when was my
heart going to get the message?

15

Tadgh pushed open the door of the Anchor and we walked inside together. Although it had been several years since I was last here, its peaty smell was still familiar to my nostrils. I looked around. The décor hadn't changed a bit. Skipper the dog raised his head from the flagstones to check who had come in then lowered it again once his curiosity had been satisfied.

'I can't believe Skipper is still alive!' I remarked as we made our way to the bar. 'He's ancient!'

'Do you remember the day Jim rescued him from the sea after some idiot had tied a rock around his neck and tried to drown him?' Tadgh said.

'Oh, yes. It was all anyone talked about for weeks. He was only a tiny pup. Well, he landed on his four paws the day he met Jim.'

'Ah, if it isn't yourself!' Jim exclaimed when he saw me. His round friendly face beamed a smile. 'You're down from Dublin, then?'

'For a little while, yeah. How's Maureen?' I replied.

'She's keeping the finest,' Jim said. 'She's busy in the

B&B at this time of year, of course. She's booked out for the whole summer. How's your little one doing? Sorry, I'm terrible with names these days.'

'Lucy. She's good.'

'And himself – the artist fella?' Jim asked.

'Joe is fine,' I said, looking over to Skipper, who was sprawled in front of the roaring fire.

'So how long are you down for?'

'I'm not sure yet.' I traced my fingers over a knot in the mahogany wood of the bar.

'What would you like, Penny?' Tadgh asked, as if sensing my discomfort.

'I'll have a gin and tonic, please.'

'And I'll have a pint, Jim.'

'Right so,' Jim said as he began to pull Tadgh's pint of Guinness. He placed the drinks on the bar when he was finished. Tadgh paid him then we sat down in a snug.

'So how are you doing?' Tadgh began. I knew it was a loaded question.

'I'm good thanks,' I lied. I was getting really good at this. The words slipped off my tongue like butter off a knife.

Tadgh paused. 'Look, Penny, we go back a long way. You don't have to put on a brave face for me.'

'What are you talking about?' I asked, suddenly feeling uncomfortable.

He took a sip from his creamy pint. 'I know about you and Joe—'

Anger rose within me. 'What do you mean?'

'Your mother told me,' he confessed, not meeting my eyes.

'She did what?' I felt hurt and betrayed. I could imagine them having a chat about me, their heads tilted in concern, saying things like, 'Ah, poor Penny, she didn't see it coming at all' or 'Pat and I always knew he'd do something like this to her. We never liked him. We tried to warn her...'. My cheeks burned with shame.

'Look, don't be angry with her,' Tadgh pleaded, placing his pint on the table. 'She didn't go into all the gory details. She's concerned about you, that's all.'

Just then the reason for Tadgh's persistence about us going for a drink together began to click into place. It had probably been Mam's idea all along.

'Was this her idea?' I snapped. 'A pity party for Penny?'

'No, of course not,' he said unconvincingly. He shifted in his seat and began to tear up his beer mat. 'I wanted to catch up with you.'

'How dare she?' I blazed.

'Please don't be mad with her,' Tadgh begged. 'She's just worried about you.'

'Well, I don't need sympathy. You don't have to stay. You can go home if you want. I'm sure you've far more important things to be doing than trying to cheer up poor Penny Murphy because her husband has left her high and dry!'

Suddenly Tadgh began to laugh. Of all the reactions he could have chosen, that was the last one I had expected. I couldn't believe his audacity.

'What are you laughing at?' I demanded.

'You haven't changed a bit,' he said, shaking his head with a grin before taking a slow sip of his pint.

'Excuse me?' I said, feeling anger course through me.

'You always were so fiery.'

I could feel my face flame. I raised my G&T to my lips and took a gulp. The alcohol burned its way down my throat. I didn't need this. I thought about getting up and leaving the pub right then, but Jim was looking over at us, probably wondering what was going on. If I stood up and walked out, I'd be the talk of the village tomorrow morning. I decided I would finish my drink, then I could leave without raising any eyebrows.

'Ah Penny, I'm only having a laugh with you,' Tadgh cajoled. 'Look, you don't need to tell me the ins and outs. It's none of my business what is happening between you and Joe—'

'You're right, it is none of your business,' I interrupted him.

'Look, Pen, we go back a long way. I don't want to fall out with you.'

It was the way he shortened my name that got me. *Pen.* He was the only person who'd ever called me that, and suddenly I was back to being a teenager again. I looked up at him and our eyes locked. I could see the familiar specks of hazel in their blue depths. I had once known those eyes better than I knew my own.

'I'm sorry,' I mumbled. 'I shouldn't have snapped at you like that.'

'It's okay. I just want you to know that I'm here for you, if you need to talk or whatever. I mean it. Break-ups are hard.' He paused before adding, 'I should know.'

There was an unmistakable hurt in his eyes, and guilt crawled through me as I thought back to our own break-up. But we had been too young to deal with the responsibility that had been thrust on us. I looked away and began to run my finger down through the condensation on the side of my glass.

'We had a lot of fun though, didn't we?' I said, trying to lighten the mood. 'Remember the time Barry Mangan played a knick-knack on Ida's door and we were convinced for weeks afterwards she was after putting a curse on us...'

He laughed. 'God, I think I slept with the light on for a

whole month after that! What about the time we all went skinny-dipping off the pier and Skipper ran off with our clothes?'

I burst out laughing, sending a spray of wine out of my mouth. 'I had forgotten about that.' We had dared each other to do it, but afterwards we couldn't find our clothes anywhere. It was only when Tadgh spotted Skipper running up the main street with his boxer shorts in his mouth that we realised what had happened. We had eventually found our clothes scattered all over the village. 'That was fun trying to explain to Mam and Dad why we were running around without a stitch on us.'

Soon we were laughing so much that my anger began to dissipate. We chatted and joked easily together as we caught up on old times. When Jim finally called last orders, I had a pain in my side from giggling at our teenage antics. It was a reminder of a time in my life when things were easy, before everything changed and we were thrown into the responsibilities of adulthood.

After we had said goodbye to Jim, we stepped outside into a clear summer evening. Stars twinkled brightly in the distance until the sky and sea merged into a navy-black on the horizon. Moths danced in the fuzzy yellow glow cast by the streetlamps on the main street. All was peaceful in Inishbeg Cove.

'I have to say I actually enjoyed myself tonight, Tadgh,' I paused. 'I'm sorry for my outburst earlier.'

'Well now, you see? I'm not the worst person to be stuck with for a few hours.'

'I'm just glad it didn't go on any longer.'

He elbowed me playfully. We had reached my door, and I was instantly transported back to all those evenings standing in the warm summer air, where he would kiss me in this exact spot, and I would pray that my parents weren't looking through the window at us.

'Are you working tomorrow?' he asked.

I nodded.

'I might drop in for a coffee if it's not too busy in the restaurant so. See you then. Goodnight, Penny.'

'Great, see you then! Goodnight, Tadgh,' I called after him, watching as his broad shape cut a path under the moonlight.

I went around to the back door, where a light was on in the kitchen. Through the glass, I saw Mam sitting at the table.

'Well?' she said before I had even closed the door behind me. She was waiting up for me, probably dying to hear how the night went.

'Well what?' I replied. I thought about my earlier anger at how she'd tried to get Tadgh to cheer me up, then my irritation faded. Maybe she had been right. I had enjoyed the evening, despite my initial reservations.

'Did ye have a good night?'

'It was okay, I suppose.'

I watched her trying to mask a smile.

I climbed into bed beside Lucy and put my arm around her small body. I loved feeling the reassuring rise and fall of her ribcage underneath my palm as she breathed deeply. As I lay there, I felt strangely light. I realised it was the first night since I had arrived in the village that I wouldn't cry myself to sleep. Suddenly everything didn't seem so bleak, and I began to think that I might just be okay.

16

The sink was full of tins, and pots and pans of different sizes, and I was elbow-deep in suds, scrubbing them clean. I had just said goodbye to Greg's father, Albie, who had joined us for dinner. Greg was dropping him back to Grovetown Nursing Home while I tidied up after dinner.

Albie and Greg had grown close in recent months. I knew Greg enjoyed spending time with his birth father, and through Albie's stories and memories Greg was able to get a sense of the person his biological mother, Della, had been. We loved hearing her brought to life.

'That was a lovely afternoon,' Greg said when he returned home a short while later. 'Albie said to tell you that he really enjoyed it.'

'I'm so glad he's in your life, Greg.' I reached out and gave his hand a squeeze.

'Me too. Life has a funny way of finding what we need when we don't even realise we're missing it.'

I opened a cupboard, took down a bowl and began to pour myself a large bowl of cornflakes.

'You're not still hungry?' Greg asked. I had just inhaled a sizeable portion of the dinner Greg had made, then had eaten the leftovers too. Thankfully, my morning sickness had recently started to ease, but now my appetite was off the scale. I couldn't seem to get enough food into me.

'It's for the babies,' I said through a mouthful.

He came over and put his arms around my waist. 'I can't wait to see them at the scan tomorrow.'

My heart flipped once more as I thought about my next hospital check-up. I always got anxious before them. I was so nervous, and just wanted everything to be okay with my babies. We were in the hospital for check-ups so frequently that we'd almost worn a path in the road, but all was going well with the pregnancy. I had passed the halfway mark, and I could hardly believe we had got so far without any drama. My check-ups were remarkably routine. Dr McCabe had even begun talking to us about our plans for the birth. It felt as though we had been given a green light: if Dr McCabe thought everything looked good and was talking about delivery dates, then I could allow myself to think about the future. Greg had even started suggesting baby names, but I wasn't quite there yet. I wouldn't relax until I was holding my babies in my arms.

'I just hope she doesn't weigh me!' My stomach had grown at an alarming rate and I'd had to give in to the heavenly comfort of maternity clothes with elasticated waistbands several weeks back. I wasn't sure whether my bump was made up of babies or food.

'Well, in that case you probably won't want this,' he said, walking over to the freezer and producing a tub of ice cream with his logo emblazoned along the side.

'Rum and raisin?' I asked, ditching the bowl of cornflakes in the sink.

'It sure is.'

'My favourite.' I sighed, shaking my head, knowing that it was futile even trying to resist it. I couldn't get enough of it these days. I had warned Greg to stop feeding my habit, but he insisted on keeping a supply of it for me in our freezer. I snatched it out of his hands, salivating before I even opened the lid. 'You can take the rap with Dr McCabe tomorrow if they need a winch to get me on the scales,' I warned.

'I love seeing you getting bigger. It means our twins are both growing away in there,' Greg said.

I flopped down on the sofa with my ice cream. I lay back against the cushions, and my bump stuck up in front of me, as round as a basketball. It was getting bigger by the day. I hadn't seen my feet in weeks, and Greg had to pull me out of my chair whenever I needed to get up. One of the twins seemed to be sitting on my bladder, so I was constantly running to the toilet. It was tricky when I was in the post office and there was a queue, but the villagers were very accommodating of my sudden need to dash off to the bathroom.

Greg joined me on the couch. I snuggled in towards him and he placed a hand on my bump, as he usually did when we watched TV in the evenings.

'How are Trouble 1 and Trouble 2 doing today?' Greg asked.

'They've been a little quiet, actually,' I remarked. 'But wait until I finish this ice cream, it'll be like *Riverdance* in a few minutes. By the way, I forgot to mention to you that the festival committee were wondering if you would like to have a stand selling your ice cream this year.'

The Inishbeg Cove Summer Festival was the highlight of the village calendar, rivalled only by the Christmas Eve carol service in St Brigid's church.

'Really?' Greg asked, surprised. 'That would be amazing.'

'I thought you'd be happy. It'll be a nice way of getting word out about the ice-cream parlour. I'll be on face-painting duty again.'

Greg's brow furrowed in concern. 'Do you really think you should do it this year?'

'Of course – why not?'

'Well, it might be a bit much with being pregnant and everything.'

'But I do it every year – who else will do it?'

'There must be someone else in the village who can paint a few butterflies or tigers, Sarah,' Greg protested.

'I know, but I enjoy doing it. I think I get as much out of it as the kids do.' I loved seeing the happy faces of the village children when I held a mirror up to their transformed faces afterwards.

'You're right. I'm sorry for being over-cautious, it's just for once in my life everything is going right. I've never been so happy, and I don't want anything to go wrong.'

Greg was usually so positive and upbeat; I wasn't used to seeing this side of him. I guessed he was worried too. Neither of us would relax until our babies were safely here.

17

PENNY

While Lucy ate breakfast in the kitchen with Mam, I took my time applying make-up in the bathroom mirror. I badly needed something to hide the dark circles from my fitful sleep the night before. It was the first time I had put on make-up since I had returned to Inishbeg Cove. I usually loved the ritual of filling in my brows and applying foundation to make my skin appear fresh and dewy, but I had lost the heart for it since I had left Dublin.

Although I had enjoyed myself in the pub, I had been feeling unsettled ever since. As Tadgh and I had chatted and laughed together, it felt like nothing had ever changed between us. And something about that had made me lie awake for most of the night, thinking. Maybe it was the alcohol, but I was pretty sure a flicker of the old spark still smouldered, and that troubled me. Although Joe and I were going through a difficult patch, I still hoped everything would work out for us. Tadgh and I may have been teenage sweethearts, but we had grown into different people and it baffled me how we had been able to take up where we left off all those years ago. Being in his company felt easy – a bit too easy.

'You're looking good,' Ruairí remarked when I came into the café later that day.

'Am I?' I was caught off guard by the compliment.

He nodded.

'It's probably just my make-up,' I said, suddenly feeling self-conscious. I must have looked a wreck without it, I thought, feeling mortified.

'By the way, I wanted to ask a favour.'

'Go on.'

'Well, you know the village festival is coming up soon? I was wondering if you'll still be around.'

'I should be – why?' The more days that passed, the less likely the idea of returning to Dublin seemed to be.

'I was wondering if perhaps you'd be able to give me a hand on the stand for the day.'

'Of course,' I said, hooking my apron around my neck. 'It's not like I'll be doing anything else. I'm sure Mam and Dad will look after Lucy.'

'You're a life-saver!' Ruairí said gratefully.

I began cleaning tables to get ready for the lunchtime rush that would soon descend upon us, but every time the bell above the door tinkled, my stomach lurched. I couldn't understand why, until I realised with some confusion that I was hoping to see Tadgh come through the door and I was disappointed every time it wasn't him. This was ridiculous, I told myself. I needed to cop myself on and stop all this madness.

The bell sounded once more and my heart soared as I turned to see who it was, but it dropped yet again when it wasn't Tadgh.

'Penny Murphy!' a voice exclaimed behind me. 'Is that you?'

I turned to see old Mrs Manning coming slowly through the door. She had grown old and frail since I had last seen her, and now used a walking stick to get around, but she still coloured her hair a vibrant shade of saffron and wore a full face of make-up. When I was growing up, I had loved her joie de vivre – she was always a colourful figure in the village.

'Great to see you, Mrs Manning. I see you're still as glam as ever.'

'Oh, you are very kind, dear. I can barely find my eyes in my falling face these days, but one must try.'

I couldn't help laughing.

'So, what has you back in the village?'

'I'm just back for a few weeks.'

If she was wondering why the hell I was working in the café when I was only visiting for a few weeks, to her credit she didn't show it.

'And did you bring that devilishly handsome artist husband with you?'

'No,' I said, feeling a wave of sadness flood me at the mention of Joe.

'More's the pity – we could do with a bit of excitement around these parts. Well, it's good to see you, Penny.' She shuffled over towards a table and Ruairí began to prepare her tea in her very own china cup, which she left in the café especially.

It was after half one when I finally saw Tadgh come through the door. My heart picked up speed at the sight of him, dressed simply in a T-shirt, shorts and flip-flops. His hair glistened with water droplets and his skin was fresh and alive.

I told myself to get it together. I was still married, for God's sake. I just couldn't understand my feelings for him. Tadgh belonged to a different time in my life. Just because I was feeling vulnerable right now, my feelings were all jumbled up.

'Were you crab fishing?' I asked. My mind had gone blank and I couldn't think of anything else to say.

He nodded. 'I've just landed my haul for the day. Last night was fun, wasn't it?' He grinned at me and I felt heat creep into my face.

'I enjoyed it,' I agreed.

'We should do it again sometime. Maybe before you go back to Dublin.'

What did that mean? 'Sometime' sounded very casual, like in the distant future. Surely he would suggest a time and date if he really wanted to see me again? Maybe he *had* just been taking pity on me, doing Mam a favour by taking me out.

'Yeah, why not?' I said, trying to sound as casual as he was. Silence fell between us and I desperately wished I could think of something witty to say. Although conversation the night before had flowed, now in the cold light of day it just felt awkward.

'Can I have an Americano to go, please?' he asked eventually.

'Sure, coming right up.' I cringed at my sing-song voice. What was wrong with me?

After my shift had ended, Ruairí sent me home with a large wedge of his divine clementine cake. We said goodbye and, as I walked along the footpath towards my parents' house, I fished my phone out of my bag. I saw I had a missed call from Joe. My heart began to pound at the sight of his name. I hated the effect he still had on me. He had left no message, so there was no way for me to gauge what he had wanted. I guessed he was probably just checking on Lucy. I took a deep breath and, instead of continuing towards Mam and Dad's house, I crossed the road and stood in front of the sea wall, looking out across the cove. The waves crashed and roared, battering the reddish stone of the headland as I dialled his number and held my breath, waiting for him to pick up.

'Penny,' he said when he finally answered.

'Hi, Joe.'

'How's Lucy doing?' His voice sounded tired and strained. I wondered if he was finding this whole thing as difficult as I was.

'She's great.'

'Does she miss me?'

'She needs to see her dad, Joe, it's been over two months.'

'Well, that's why I was calling. I was hoping you could bring her to see me.'

I was stunned by his audacity. 'Can't you come here?' Although I did need to go back to the house we shared, after two months apart I wasn't going to jump to his orders.

'Don't be difficult, Penny. You're the one who left our home.'

'Only because you gave me no option!' My voice cracked, allowing emotion to seep through.

'You can't keep her away from me!' he warned.

'I'm not, Joe. You know where we are if you want to see us,' I said.

The line went dead. He had hung up on me. I gripped the phone with trembling hands. Why did he always have this effect on me?

'Are you okay?' I heard a voice say from behind.

I swung around, quickly wiping away the tears from my eyes. It was Tadgh.

I tried to compose myself. 'It's nothing,' I said, avoiding eye contact.

He nodded, but I could tell he wasn't buying it. 'Want to take a walk?'

I shook my head. 'I can't. I have to get back to Lucy.'

'Well, how about I walk you home then?'

I couldn't help smiling at him. It was as if he knew when I needed someone. 'Thanks, Tadgh.'

'Is everything okay?' he asked as we walked along the main street.

'No,' I said shaking my head, feeling fresh tears pulse in my eyes. 'It's a mess. Why is love so hard?'

'It doesn't have to be, Penny. You know he shouldn't be making you feel this way.'

'I don't think I can be at the mercy of his moods any more.'

'It sounds like it's about time you stopped letting him treat you like a doormat. You were always so sparky. Where's that girl gone?'

He was right, where was that girl gone? The one who wasn't afraid of being pushed away or waiting for the right mood? The old Penny would never have settled for being treated like this. How had I become this person? A person whose happiness was dependent on the moods and dramas of somebody else? I barely recognised myself any more. I guess it had crept up on me over the years, but somewhere along the line I had changed, and it wasn't for the better.

'I don't know.' I sighed sadly. 'I don't know when or how it happened but I'm not *me* any more.'

'Well, let's get you back then,' he said with a grin, and I couldn't help smile back at him.

'Do you want to come in for a cuppa?' I asked when we reached my parents' cottage. 'Ruairí has given me a big wedge of his clementine cake.'

He shook his head. 'I'd better get up to the restaurant. I've been gone for long enough – they'll be wondering where I got to. Thanks anyway.'

I didn't go into the house immediately. Instead I watched him walk off towards the cliff path. I couldn't help thinking about his words.

New hope flickered inside me. I was broken and fractured right now but, after spending time with Tadgh, I was reminded of the old me. Maybe that girl was finally starting to emerge again.

18

SARAH

I pulled open the curtains and held my breath. It was the morning of the village festival. I breathed a sigh of relief when I looked out to see strong sunlight glinting like platinum off the sea. There wasn't a whisper of wind, and fleecy clouds trailed delicately on an azure backdrop where seagulls arced gracefully. The weather gods had smiled on the village. The weather could make or break the festival – I recalled many years where the rain had teemed down all day and the whole thing was a washout. The other villagers would all breathe a huge sigh of relief when they opened their curtains and saw blue skies and sunshine.

As well as traditional funfair games like hoopla and ring-a-duck, there would be stalls selling bric-a-brac and handmade crafts, as well as homemade goods and preserves. Ruairí would be selling his baked goods and teas and coffees, and for the first year Greg would have an ice-cream stall, which I knew was going to be a big hit, especially on a sunny day like today. Mr Galvin would be leading pony rides up and down the beach, I was on face-painting duty, and

Senan O'Reilly was going to run a limbo competition for the teenagers. The day always culminated in a firework show over the cove just after sunset. People came from far and wide around the county: it was a great day in the village.

I had so many happy memories of the Inishbeg Cove Summer Festival from childhood. As a teenager, when I was too old for pony rides and face painting, a gang of us would sit up on the rocks and watch the fireworks after the sun had gone down.

I got into the shower and noticed that my bump seemed to have grown even bigger overnight. I'd never thought it was possible for a human to expand so rapidly but I guessed it meant the babies were happy. After I was finished, I dressed and came downstairs to the delicious aroma of fried bacon.

'Good morning, beautiful,' Greg said when I entered the living area. 'Did you sleep well?' His eyes landed on the box of face paints I was carrying for the festival. 'Do you really think you should be lifting that?' His brow was furrowed in concern.

'It's only a small box, Greg,' I said putting it down on the table.

'Are you sure you should be doing it?' he asked me once again. 'Nobody would mind if you took a rain check.'

'It's hardly taxing. I'll be sitting down all day.'

'Well, promise me you'll take it easy, okay? If at any point you feel like it's getting too much, just give me a wave and I'll try and distract the little brats with some free ice cream or something.'

I laughed.

'And I'm carrying that box,' he said.

'Yes, sir!' I saluted him.

'This isn't funny, Sarah. I just want what's best for you and our babies.'

I knew this was just Greg's way of being in control of a scary situation. He went back and flipped over the sizzling bacon in the frying pan. 'Just think, in a couple of years we'll have two little faces of our own queuing up, begging to be painted,' Greg said.

My stomach constricted, as it always did whenever I thought about the future. I was glad that Greg had chosen to stay in his bubble of bliss, where everything was going to work out okay, because it meant he was protected from the worries that now consumed my every waking hour. Greg had already planned a future for our babies, whereas I was still taking it day by day. I took a deep breath to calm myself. A few months ago, I never could have imagined being pregnant with one baby, let alone with twins. Now that it had happened, I loved them both dearly. Although I hadn't met them yet, they were already a huge part of my life and I couldn't imagine how I would cope if anything went wrong.

Greg served me a plate of crispy bacon on thickly sliced soda bread oozing with golden butter. It wasn't the healthiest breakfast option, but it was a Saturday morning treat. I spotted Gareth, the stray tabby cat who seemed to have adopted Greg and me, sitting on the windowsill. He was waiting for leftovers – he always timed his visits with our mealtimes.

After I had polished off my breakfast, I was getting up from the table when I felt a flutter, as light as butterfly wings. My heart swelled. I loved feeling my babies move – it reassured me. I had been feeling them a lot lately, and their movements were getting stronger with every passing day.

'What is it?' Greg asked looking at me, his face concerned.

'I guess the babies must like bacon.' I laughed. 'Here, see if you can feel it too.'

I lifted my T-shirt and Greg placed the palm of his hand on my abdomen. Instantly, like a flick against taut elastic, there was another kick.

'Did you feel that?' I said.

Greg looked back at me with the broadest smile. 'Well done, Greg Juniors.'

'Or they could be Sarah Juniors.' I laughed. 'Now come on. We'd better go, or I'll have a queue of angry children waiting for me.'

The day of the Inishbeg Cove Summer Festival had finally arrived, and Ruairí and I were in the kitchen baking up a storm. Our stand was going to sell teas, coffees and sweet treats, and we had been working long hours that week to get everything ready.

I rose early that morning, leaving Lucy to snooze for longer. I dressed, then hurried the short distance from the cottage to the café in the cool morning air. I was relieved to see that the sun was out, and it looked like it was going to be a glorious day. I couldn't remember ever having bad weather at the festival; maybe I was looking back through rose-tinted glasses, but the sun always seemed to shine on festival day.

When I went through the café door, the air was scented with sweet summer berries and zesty lemon. I followed the aroma and found Ruairí in the kitchen in a cloud of icing sugar. An oven was beeping, and several trays of scones were sitting on the counter, waiting to be loaded.

'Penny! Thank goodness you're here,' he said, relief flooding his face. 'That oven is about to incinerate those scones and I've three hundred cupcakes that need to be iced.'

'I'm on it!' I said, hurrying over and silencing the beeping. I took the trays of golden scones out of the oven before loading it up with the next batch. Then, while the scones were cooling, I picked up the icing bag and began to decorate the cupcakes. The festival wasn't due to start until three o'clock, but we had a lot to do before then.

WE HAD JUST FINISHED SETTING up our displays of cupcakes and putting the finishing touches to the stand when we were descended upon by festival goers. Ruairí and I barely had time to breathe as we served customer after customer.

When we finally had a lull and I had a chance to look up, I saw villagers sitting around the sand on deckchairs and rugs, eating picnics, while Mr Galvin led children up and down the beach on a dun-coloured pony. A child who had won a teddy in the hoopla was holding it above his head like a trophy. Sarah had a steady stream of kids waiting patiently for face painting, and Greg's ice-cream stall had a never-ending queue too. I spotted Lucy in the distance, chasing a group of similar-aged children through the dunes. It was lovely to watch her having so much fun. It reminded me of my own childhood and all the fun I had had on festival day as I tore around the beach making new friends.

As dusk began to fall over the cove, the stallholders started to pack up while the villagers waited for the firework display to begin.

'Aw, don't tell me all the cupcakes have been sold,' said a familiar voice just as I was boxing up whatever we had left.

I looked up to see Tadgh standing before me.

'I do have a unicorn one left,' I offered.

'It'll have to do, I suppose.' He pouted playfully as I used tongs to place the cake in a paper bag for him.

'That was a great day,' I said, looking around at the crowded beach.

'You can't beat festival day in Inishbeg Cove,' Tadgh said, following my gaze. 'It's the best day of the year.'

He gave Ruairí a hand dismantling the stand, while I made trips between the beach and the café to bring back all of our equipment. On one of my many trips back, I saw Mam and Dad further up the cove with Lucy sandwiched between them, making their way towards us. They were walking along, each holding one of Lucy's hands, and every now and then they swung her between them. It was heartwarming to watch them. This was by far the longest period of time Lucy had spent in Inishbeg Cove – my visits home with her were usually fleeting weekend affairs, but since we had come here nearly three months ago, my parents and Lucy had developed a special bond. They adored spending time with her – so much so that I was dreading telling her we'd have to leave. I had noticed that recently they had stopped asking me when I was going home. I didn't know if it was because they didn't want to pry, or because they were afraid of what my answer would be.

'Mama!' Lucy cried, letting go of her grandparents' hands and running over to me. I scooped my daughter into my arms and sat her on my hip. I wiped a smudge of chocolate ice cream from her nose before leaning in to kiss it.

'Did you have fun today?'

She nodded then yawned, her mouth stretching in a perfect circle.

'Somebody's tired.' Tadgh nodded at her as he handed a pole to Ruairí.

'Me not tired,' Lucy replied defiantly.

'That's me told!' Tadgh laughed.

'I don't think she'll last until the fireworks. I should probably take her home,' I said.

'I'll take her,' Mam offered. 'Why don't you stay on? You've worked hard today.'

'Are you sure you don't mind?' It had been a great day and I didn't want it to end just yet.

'Sure, she's no trouble at all.' Mam patted Lucy's soft curls with the palm of her hand. 'Anyway, I'd say she'll be asleep before her head hits the pillow.'

I kissed Lucy goodbye and my parents took her home.

After we had brought all the equipment back to the café, Ruairí surprised Tadgh and me by producing a wicker picnic basket.

'Ta-da!' he said with a flourish as he took out a bottle of prosecco. 'I think we deserve this!' He pulled the cork, causing the golden liquid to froth over the neck of the bottle, before pouring generous glasses for us all.

'I don't think I've ever been as glad to see alcohol,' I said, taking a sip.

We climbed up onto a large rock. I sighed in relief to finally be sitting down. My feet were burning, and my legs ached from the non-stop running back and forth between the stall and the café.

'This is very fancy,' Tadgh said as Ruairí produced a box of crackers and cheeses from the basket and began to serve them.

'Well, my motto is, if you're going to do something in life, you may as well do it well,' Ruairí said.

We toasted one another – 'Here's to a great festival!' – and clinked glasses. Suddenly there was a loud burst of noise, and the navy-blue sky was streaked in all the colours of the rainbow. We sipped prosecco as the fireworks screamed through the air and exploded in a riot of vibrant hues against the dark sky. It was as if an artist had been let loose with his paints. Even though the day had been hectic, and my body was aching, I had enjoyed it immensely. I felt a huge sense of satisfaction at a job well done. The festival had been a success and I had played a part – albeit very small – in it. It had been a long time since I had felt a similar sense of achievement. I was proud to have been involved. I had witnessed more community spirit among the villagers in one afternoon than I had in all my years living in Dublin. I had loved watching the older people relax in their deckchairs for the day and to see the young children, including my daughter, running around, having hours of carefree fun on the sand. It was nice to belong again. I realised that, for the first time in a long time, I was contented. I was content here in this moment, watching the fireworks, drinking prosecco and eating delicious cheese with two men who had become good friends to me over the last few weeks.

After the fireworks had ended and the sky had been restored to its usual blanket of ombré shades of navy, sprinkled with perfect jewel stars, people began to pack up around us and the beach was tranquil once more.

'I don't know about you two, but I'm bushed,' Ruairí said, letting out a bear-like yawn. 'Thanks for today, Penny. I would have been lost without you.' He planted a kiss on my cheek before climbing down from the rock. 'I'll be off.' He gathered up his basket and headed off, leaving Tadgh and me alone together.

'I really enjoyed myself today,' I said, turning to Tadgh. 'It took me right back to all the festivals I've gone to over the years since I was Lucy's age.'

'Do you remember the year you, June Eivers and Laura McPolin formed a band?' Tadgh said.

'Oh, please don't remind me!' I laughed. 'I think I had suppressed that memory.'

'Didn't you call yourselves the Backstreet *Girls*?' he taunted.

'Hey! We were very original!' I said in mock defence. I cringed as I recalled how we had begged the organising committee to allow us to perform our first gig at the festival. 'We took it so seriously – we rehearsed every day after school in Laura's bedroom. We really believed that we'd get a record deal, but we just went blank when we got up on the stage. I don't think I'll ever live that down.'

Tadgh was bent double in laughter at the memory. 'I think every child has a horror story from the festival. I remember one year when it rained non-stop. I reckon I was about five or six, and Mam had painted my face as Spider-man, except she decided to use normal paint – no way was she going to waste any money on fancy face paint. Anyway, it all washed off in the rain and red paint was running in rivers down my face, down my clothes – everything I touched was destroyed. It was everywhere. It was like a scene from a horror movie.'

We were in hysterics as we recalled our festival memories. I liked how being in Tadgh's company made me feel – as if I was important to him. He listened to me when I talked. Really listened. We could laugh and have fun together and I wasn't second-guessing myself, wondering how he would react or twist every innocent little thing I said.

'You see?' Tadgh said after a while. 'Inishbeg Cove isn't the worst place to be.' He grinned.

'No, it's not,' I found myself agreeing with him. 'I think,

in all my time in Dublin, I'd forgotten all the good things about belonging in a village.'

'So, have you decided when you're going back yet?' Tadgh asked.

I shook my head. 'I honestly don't know what I'm doing.' I sighed. 'Joe is giving me a hard time about not seeing Lucy, but I can't help thinking that if he really wants to see her then he should be willing to get in the car and drive here.'

'You'd think so,' Tadgh replied.

'I don't want to play games or be stubborn or make this situation any harder than it already is – Lucy needs her dad – but do you know something, Tadgh?' I turned to face him. 'I think I'm tired of dancing to Joe de Paor's tune.'

'I think that's very wise.'

I suddenly shivered in the cool evening air. Tadgh took off his jacket and put it around my shoulders. 'It's getting chilly. We should probably be getting home,' he said, climbing down from the rock.

I went to get up too and found I barely had the energy to move; I had survived on adrenalin all day and now tiredness was hitting me like a wall. Tadgh offered me his hand to help me down onto the sand and we strolled back up the deserted beach together. Moonlight bathed the sand silver and cast a path across the sea. The softly breaking waves rushing up the beach provided the backdrop to our conversation.

'It's a pity we have to grow up and have responsibilities. I wish we could have stayed carefree teenagers forever,' I said feeling wistful.

Tadgh looked out at the ocean. 'It wasn't all fun and games back then...' He trailed off and instantly the atmosphere had changed.

'You're right, I'm so sorry,' I said, abashed. I shook my

head at my carelessness. I had been completely insensitive. What Tadgh had gone through was a living nightmare for anyone, but to experience a tragedy of that magnitude at such a tender age must have been unbearable. I could still remember the visceral sense of shock and raw grief felt by the whole community. Everyone had been stunned by the loss of his parents and by how a person's world could be turned upside-down in a second.

'You must really miss them,' I said, rubbing his arm.

'Every single day. I still wonder what my life might have been like if they hadn't been taken so young ... how things might have worked out.'

Our eyes met and I guessed he was thinking about our teenage love.

'I know we were only teenagers,' he continued, 'but we were so good together, you and me. When you broke up with me that day in the cove, I thought my world had ended.'

'Really?' I was shocked by his admission. For years I had thought breaking up with me was what he wanted.

'I didn't see it coming,' he went on.

'I never wanted to break up with you, Tadgh.'

'Well then, why did you do it?'

'You had so much on your plate after your parents died, with Senan and the restaurant, and I thought I was getting in your way...'

'I thought you didn't love me any more.'

I shook my head. 'I was devastated, Tadgh. I thought if I suggested we take a break, it would make you realise how far we had slipped away from one another, but then when you agreed that we should go our separate ways, I was heart-broken. I assumed it was what you wanted but you'd been too afraid to tell me.'

'I never wanted to lose you, Penny. I really believed you wanted to head off to college in Dublin like a normal teenager without any of the hassle that had landed on my doorstep, and I wouldn't blame you for that. I should have been honest and fought harder for you, but I was still trying to get my head around losing my parents. I guess my pride was trying to protect me from any more pain...'

'We were so young, Tadgh. We thought we had life all figured out ... but we hadn't a clue.' I looked out over the water.

'Do you ever wonder what would have happened if we had stayed together?' he asked. As his bright eyes searched my face, I could see pain in their depths.

I bent down and picked up a pebble and cast it into the inky water. 'Honestly? Not really. We were just kids.'

'But what if the timing or circumstances were different? I wonder, would things have worked out for us?'

I shrugged. 'Who knows? Maybe we would have stayed together and have had ten children, or maybe we would still have broken up eventually. It's not *Sliding Doors* – we don't get to watch the other version of our lives.'

'In some ways, being with you now, it's almost like we've never been apart.'

I knew what he meant. Since I had bumped into him on the beach with Lucy that day, it was as if we had taken straight up from where we had left off all those years ago. To Tadgh, I was my younger self: I was young, fun-loving, fear-less Penny. I wasn't the woman who no longer knew who she was or where she belonged. I missed the safety of our teenage days and the version of me that Tadgh had loved. I wanted to be that girl once more. Suddenly I longed for the familiarity of his touch. I found myself reaching forward and cupping his face in my hands. I tilted my face up towards his and waited to feel the reassurance of his soft lips against mine. I searched for the mouth I had once known so well, but his lips weren't there. Instead, I was met with cold air as Tadgh pulled back from me.

Immediately I dropped my hands and stepped back from him.

'Penny, I'm sorry,' he said, not looking me in the eye.

'It's okay. I shouldn't have done that – I don't know what came over me.' I was mortified. *Damn it to hell, what was I thinking?* Even though Joe and I were going through a difficult patch, we were still *married*. The prosecco had obviously gone straight to my head. I began to hurry towards the path through the dunes that led back up to the village. Tadgh strode after me.

'I'd better go. Mam is probably waiting up for me,' I said when we had reached the main street. The place was quiet; everyone was tucked up in bed after the festivities.

'I'll walk you home.'

'No, honestly, it's okay,' I mumbled without meeting his eye. I turned away from him. His rejection was almost worse than my embarrassment at my attempted kiss. I could feel it burn its way down inside me, crawling around underneath my skin.

'Penny, wait—' he called after me as I hurried down the main street towards my parents' house, but I had to escape from him – and my humiliation.

I was sitting on the kitchen floor beside Lucy, who was pouring imaginary teas and coffees into tiny china teacups. Mam had bought the red polka-dot tea set in O'Herlihy's and Lucy's new favourite game was playing 'Ruairí's café'.

'This a for you, Mama.' She handed me a delicate cup balanced precariously on a matching saucer.

'Oh, thank you, Lucy Lu,' I said, pretending to take a sip.

'This a for you, Ganny,' she said, standing up and handing a cup to my mother, who was sitting at the kitchen table. 'And this for you, Gandad.' Carefully she carried a cup over to my father.

'This is delicious tea, Lucy,' my father said.

Lucy turned back to me. 'Drink your tea, Mama,' she scolded.

'Sorry,' I said, raising the cup to my lips again.

'You'll need to start thinking about playschools if you're still here come September,' Mam reminded me once again.

The days were going so fast. It was hard to believe that September was a little more than a month away. Even though I was doing nothing to further my move back to Dublin, I still couldn't imagine myself being here in a month's time.

'Josephine has a lovely little playgroup,' Mam continued, nodding at Lucy who was playing, blissfully unaware of the topic of conversation. 'Missy would be in her element there.'

'Has Josephine not retired yet?' I asked. She had been my playschool teacher almost thirty years ago.

'Not yet. I can have a word with her to see if she'd have a place for Lucy?' Mam pushed, a hopeful note in her voice.

'I'm not sure...'

'You're going to have to make a decision soon, Penny,' Mam warned. 'You can't keep living in limbo, not knowing whether you're coming or going. It's not good for you or Lucy.'

'I know, Mam,' I replied, with a sigh of defeat. 'I know.'

'Would it really be so bad to stay in Inishbeg Cove for a few months?' Dad asked gently. He always took a softer approach than Mam.

'I just need a little longer to think about everything,' I said to appease them. No matter how hard I tried, I couldn't seem to get my head together. I felt overwhelmed; it was as if there was a rock sitting on my chest and I couldn't move out from underneath it. I was stuck there beneath its weight, unable to make a decision.

'Any word from Joe?' Mam enquired.

'Not since the other day,' I replied. He had phoned to talk to Lucy again, but she had grown distracted and wandered off in the middle of the conversation. I had tried to coax her back to talk to him, but she was three years old and didn't have the attention span yet. Mam pursed her lips in disapproval. I knew this would lead to a rant about Joe, and I just couldn't listen to it right now.

'I'd better get ready for work,' I said, getting up from the floor, eager to escape their inquisition.

LATER THAT AFTERNOON, Ruairí and I were working flat out in the café. From the moment I had stepped inside the door, customers had been arriving thick and fast. There was no let-up in the lunchtime rush. They were mainly holiday-makers and day-trippers making the most of the last days of summer before the cooler weather made its presence felt, but some of the villagers were there too, like the sea swim-mers and Mrs Manning, who was sipping tea from her cup, which was circled with a ring of red lipstick.

Sunlight cast an ochre light through the windows. Although the day was sunny, a cool south-westerly breeze was coming in off the Atlantic so only a few hardy souls dared to sit outside, which made the café feel even busier.

We served endless sandwiches, panini and salads, scones and cakes until my head was spinning and my hands felt as though I could butter bread in my sleep. Eventually the customers began to slow to a steady trickle and Ruairí and I had time to catch our breath.

I was clearing off a table when a voice called from behind me. 'Penny, can I talk to you for a minute?'

I swung around to see Tadgh standing there. Mortifica-tion wormed its way through my body.

'Sure,' I said, piling dirty plates and mugs on the tray.

I had gone home the night of the festival feeling ashamed. All weekend, I cringed at myself for being so stupid. I still didn't know what had come over me. What had I been thinking, leaning in to kiss him like that? Was it simply the deadly combination of exhaustion and too much alcohol? Or perhaps I was feeling nostalgic after another beautiful summer festival, or maybe it was because my self-worth was on the floor and Tadgh's familiarity was easy and appealing. I guessed it was probably a combination of all three reasons. But try as I might, I couldn't figure it out. I was so confused by my actions, so God only knew how Tadgh was feeling.

The thing was, I didn't even like him in that way. It was as though I had taken a leave of absence from my body. I had thought about calling him, but humiliation had stopped me. Things were bad enough without me digging an even bigger hole. Knowing me, if I picked up the phone to try and explain it, I would probably end up making everything worse.

Tadgh looked across to Ruairí, who was standing watching us from behind the counter.

'In private?' Tadgh mumbled.

'Well, I'm busy...' Mrs Manning was staring at us from across the café, not bothering to disguise her interest. She was clearly enjoying the drama, which added to my embarrassment.

'Why don't you two nip into the kitchen for a moment?' Ruairí suggested.

I knew he was just trying to be helpful, but this was going to be beyond awkward.

'Okay.' My heart was beating so loudly that I was sure Tadgh could hear it as he followed me.

'So, what's up?' I asked when we were alone together. I was doing my utmost to sound nonchalant, even though I felt anything but.

He stood there looking sheepish. Was he finding this just as embarrassing as I was? A stray curl had fallen across one eye, and I resisted the urge to reach across and push it away. He smoothed it back off his face, but it sprang out from behind his ear again. His hair always had a mind of its own.

'I just wanted to apologise—' he began.

'You've nothing to apologise for.'

'Well, then I think I should explain—'

'You don't need to explain,' I said, cutting him off again.

'Will you just hear me out, Penny, for God's sake?' he said with a touch of impatience. 'The other evening on the beach... I wanted to kiss you, of course I did, but...' He paused. 'Please don't take this the wrong way, but I don't think you're ready.'

His words knocked me off balance. I felt myself stumble as I tried to catch myself. 'Ready?' I blustered. 'Ready for what?'

'Well, to be with someone new.' His face changed from a light blush pink to a more intense shade of red. He was visibly squirming in front of me.

'Look, I think you're reading too much into it, Tadgh,' I said, trying to recover myself. 'I had a long day and the prosecco went to my head. Let's just forget it ever happened.'

'Oh...' he said, looking abashed. The flecks of hazel in his eyes danced as they met mine, and I found myself looking away.

'So, we're okay?' I went on.

He looked as though he was about to say something else, but changed his mind at the last minute. 'We're good,' he agreed.

'Great,' I said, forcing a smile on my face. 'Well, I'd better get back to work – there's a queue building again out there.' I began to walk out of the kitchen.

'Sure,' he said, stepping aside to let me past him.

'What was all that about?' Ruairí asked after Tadgh had

walked out without saying goodbye to him. 'He looks like he swallowed a wasp.'

'It's nothing.'

'It didn't look like nothing to me. In fact, if you ask me, it looks as though the old spark has been reignited,' he said, winking at me.

'Nobody asked you,' I quipped. 'Anyway, we're just friends. I'm still married, for God's sake, Ruairí!'

'You know what they say: the fastest way to get over someone is to get under somebody new—'

I swatted him playfully with a tea towel.

'Ow,' he said, clutching his arm dramatically and rolling around, pretending to be hurt.

I shook my head despairingly at him and went back to work cleaning down tables. Tadgh's words were still sloshing around inside my head, like a little rowing boat being battered in a storm. Even though I had feigned indifference, he had rattled me. I hadn't expected him to admit that he wanted to kiss me. Did that mean he had feelings for me? And what the hell had he meant, I wasn't ready? Of course I wasn't ready – although everyone else seemed to think I was deluded, deep in my heart a tiny flicker of hope still burned that my marriage might be salvaged.

For the next few days Tadgh didn't come in for a coffee like he usually did, and I found my days felt a little lacklustre, as if someone had twisted a dimmer switch. I hadn't realised how much I had looked forward to Tadgh's daily visits to the café. I missed seeing his friendly grin across the counter as he ordered his Americano to go, and this made me confused. Was it purely friendship or did he mean something more to me? Was Ruairí right – had the old flame between us been rekindled somewhere along the line? But no. I was married and, no matter what happened, I didn't want my marriage to be over. My feelings were all blurred and I couldn't seem to understand them, no matter how hard I tried.

I kept replaying our last conversation on a loop inside my head. Standing in the kitchen, Tadgh had bared his soul to me, but I had responded by being blasé and offhand with him, and I felt guilty for how I had handled it. When I thought back on it, he had seemed a little broken as he had walked out the door. Maybe it was my imagination, but had there been a sheen of hurt in his eyes? I recognised the look he had given me as he had turned and left the kitchen and I realised with shame that I had seen that look once before, back when we had been teenagers trying to deal with feelings and emotions that were bigger than us.

'I haven't seen Tadgh in a few days,' Ruairí remarked one day.

'Yeah,' I said, feeling my heart pick up speed at the mention of his name.

'It's strange – normally he comes in for his takeaway Americano,' he pressed.

I shrugged. 'Maybe he's just busy.'

'Hmm,' Ruairí replied with a smile. 'Something tells me you might be the reason, Penny Murphy.' He wagged his finger at me.

'It's Penny de Paor, actually. And I've no idea what you're talking about.'

INSTEAD OF GOING STRAIGHT HOME after work that day, I decided to walk up the cliff path for some fresh air to clear my head. If you ever needed space to think or to blow away the cobwebs, the cliff walk was the cure. I climbed the well-worn path leading from the village. Although the gradient wasn't overly steep, my calves were beginning to burn and I had to stop to catch my breath several times. The waves rolled against the cliffs to my left. I looked across the cove to where Tadgh's restaurant was little more than a speck on the cliff face. I imagined him busy in the kitchen, seasoning and tasting dishes to make sure they were just right, his concentration and focus intense, as it always was when it came to his restaurant.

I kept climbing until the village looked like a miniature

model below me, with matchstick people and toy cars. Then I saw Ida the herbalist coming towards me in the distance. I hadn't seen her in years. She still carried her strange staff, using it to steady herself as she descended the gravelly path. I used to be terrified of her as a child – the other children had filled my head with scary stories about her – but now I realised that, although she was a little odd, she was harmless. She stopped and bent to pick some wildflowers before walking on again. As she got closer to me, I could see that her face had grown more lined and weathered, giving her a wizened look. I nodded to her as we passed one another, but she didn't look at me from beneath the hood of her cloak.

I climbed higher until I finally saw the old cottage ruin in the distance. It had crumbled even more since I last saw it. We had sometimes hung out there as teenagers, but the roof had now fallen in and tufts of grass grew between the stones in its walls. I got closer to where the ground levelled off, then looked out at the wild Atlantic Ocean as it rolled into the Irish coastline. Wispy clouds scudded so fast above my head, it was as if someone had pressed a fast-forward button. Standing up there, I felt as if I was on the edge of the world. It was like a metaphor for how my life was right now: I had run so far, there was nowhere left to go.

Mam's words had been playing like a stuck record inside my head for the last few days. It had been three months since I had left Dublin. Perhaps she was right. Had the time come to admit that my marriage was over? I had given Joe enough time. If he wanted us back, wouldn't he have said so by now? The one thing I knew for sure was that I couldn't keep living the way I was, without a plan for the future. Even though it would wrench my heart in two, I decided that I would return to Dublin the following weekend to collect our belongings. I would ask Joe not to be at home when I called.

It would make things too difficult. Then Lucy and I would return to Inishbeg Cove and stay in the village until I figured out what I was going to do. Having to start from scratch again was daunting but, no matter how painful it was, I needed to face up to reality – for my own sake as well as Lucy's.

I glanced at my phone and saw I had a missed call from Mam. I hadn't heard it ring over the roar of the ocean and the wind swirling in my ears. I realised she had been expecting me home nearly an hour ago and she was probably starting to worry. I fired off a quick text to say I had gone for a walk and would be back shortly, then I turned and began my descent towards the village. I knew Mam would be happy when I told her about my decision to stay in Inishbeg Cove for the foreseeable future.

I was almost at the point where the path forked: one path returned to the village, and the other cut through the dunes around the cove, eventually ending up at the restaurant. In the distance I saw the broad outline of a familiar figure coming towards me. My heart felt as though it was balancing on a tightrope. It was Tadgh.

22

I woke with a heavy, ominous feeling of dread clouding me. I couldn't explain it. Perhaps it was tiredness after the festival the previous weekend catching up with me. Although I would never admit it to Greg, it had taken more out of me than I expected. I decided not to say anything to him; he would only worry.

'What do you think of Theodore and Robert if they're boys?' Greg suggested as we ate breakfast together that morning. 'We could call them Theo and Rob for short.' He was forever suggesting baby names, whereas I hadn't wanted to think that far ahead. Greg was like an optimistic ostrich with his head stuck in the sand, shielding himself from any worries. He was convinced that everything would work out. I hated to drag him down with my anxieties so instead I tried to keep them to myself and took the pregnancy day by day.

'I like it, but I think Rum and Raisin would be better,' I said, grabbing my bag.

'Great suggestions! And that would work whether

they're girls or boys,' he said, laughing as I kissed him on the cheek before heading out the door.

No matter how hard I tried, I couldn't shake the uneasy feeling as I went about my work that day. I was sorting through a stack of letters later that morning when I felt a pain shoot through my bump. It was sudden and sharp, and made me stop and catch my breath. I had been petrified of every little twinge I felt, but the pregnancy book Greg had bought said that some cramping and twinges were normal in pregnancy, so I tried to not to worry. It was probably just tiredness from overdoing it at the festival.

I was trying to concentrate on work when I was hit by another cramp a short time later. This one was fiercer, and it felt as though my whole bump was in spasm. I had to hold on to the counter until it had passed. Another assailed me a few minutes later, and I began to worry. Was something wrong with the babies? I didn't want to panic and run to the doctor over every little twinge, but maybe I needed medical attention. It was far too soon to be labour pains. I decided to wait it out a while longer and if I still was cramping, then I would call Greg and see what he thought we should do. I didn't want to worry him unnecessarily.

I gritted my teeth through the pain and continued to serve customers. As they chatted, I tried my best to stay focused on what they were saying to me, but the cramps were getting stronger, forcing me stop every time a pain hit. I could hardly concentrate as Mrs Manning dropped off some eggs for me and filled me in on some anecdote involving hair dye and her hens. At one point I accidentally gave Timmy O'Malley the wrong change because I was so caught up in the pain.

Soon the cramping had got so bad that I could no longer

ignore it. I was gripped by wave after wave of pain. I went into the bathroom and sat on the toilet. Then I saw it. Bright red blood stained my underwear. My legs felt weak and jelly-like. Deep down, I had known this was going to happen. Everything had been going so well with the pregnancy – a bit too well. I was angry with myself. I should never have allowed myself to believe that the babies might be safe. I was stupid to get my hopes raised, only to have them dashed again.

I came out of the bathroom and grabbed my phone, fumbling as I tried to dial Greg's number.

'Sarah, is everything okay?' I could hear the ice-cream parlour jukebox playing 'Fun, Fun, Fun' by The Beach Boys and the chatter of his customers in the background. 'Sarah, are you there?' he repeated.

'You need to hurry, Greg. I think I'm losing our babies.'

Even though my head said to keep walking, my feet didn't listen. They stopped and waited for Tadgh to reach me. My heart was hammering. I racked my brain thinking of something to say to him, but all thoughts had fled. His intense blue eyes and rugged features reminded me of the rocky cliffs and crystal-clear sea that surrounded Inishbeg Cove, and his wild tangle of hair was like the wind waving through the marram grass on the dunes. It was as if he had been etched out of this landscape.

'I thought you'd be in the restaurant?' I said as he got closer.

'I needed to pick up some more ice cream from Greg.'

'Look, Tadgh, I'm sorry if I was rude in the café the other day,' I began.

'No worries.' His eyes flickered down to the grass.

'You caught me off guard. I'm feeling so confused about everything right now,' I explained.

'I get it. I think we're both feeling confused...'

'What do you mean?'

He took a deep breath and I could tell he was steeling himself for whatever he was about to say next.

'Maybe it's just me, but ever since you came back to the village, I feel that something has changed.' A note of frustration peppered his voice. 'Now maybe I'm crazy and it's all in my head, but no matter how much you deny it, I think there is something still there between us. Something I thought had burnt out a long time ago.'

I knew exactly what he was talking about. It was like the invisible force you felt when you put two magnets of the same charge together – strong and unbreakable. I couldn't lie to him; he knew me too well.

'I can feel it too,' I admitted, scared to allow myself to say it out loud. Telling him was terrifying, as if opening up a chasm of unknown depth into my heart.

'I knew it wasn't just my imagination.' His eyes met mine with brooding intensity. 'I knew you had to feel it too.' He pushed a curl back off his face. I longed to reach forward and touch it. 'But I know you still want to work things out with Joe,' he continued, 'and I would never get in the way of that—'

'Well, actually I think I've finally accepted that it's over between us,' I confessed.

There was an unmistakable flicker of hope in his slate-blue eyes, but he quickly composed his face again. 'I'm sorry to hear that, Penny.'

'Thanks, Tadgh,' I whispered, feeling a sadness weigh me down as I thought about my doomed marriage.

'Look, I know your head is all over the place right now, but ... I wanted to let you know that I'm here for you, whenever you're ready. I'll wait for you.'

His words were like a warm blanket cocooning me. Suddenly I was transported back to when we were carefree teenagers, before Tadgh's parents had been killed. Back when the village was our playground and our biggest worry was whether we could sneak out of our houses to meet down at the moonlit cove. All thoughts left my head, the roar of the crashing waves faded, until all I could hear was the blood pulsing in my ears. Everything melted away before me until it was just Tadgh and me, the way we used to be, before life got complicated. He took a step towards me and I moved closer to him until our faces were millimetres apart. Our eyes met. It felt like this was the moment we had both been waiting for: everything, all the heartache we had experienced, had led us right here, to this moment. This was the path we were destined to be on. Slowly he bent his head and began to kiss my neck, so gently it felt as though a butterfly's wing was caressing my skin. I melted against him, knowing I could fight no longer. Our lips met, warm and familiar, soothing like a balm. We kissed as if making up for all the years we had spent apart. We fell to our knees, the marram grass coarse and damp beneath us. Our kisses became more fervent with every passing second, as our bodies communicated to one another in a language only we knew.

24

I felt like skipping the whole way home to my parents' cottage. The birdsong sounded sharper and the sun shone a little brighter. I had just reached the house when Mam appeared at the front door.

'Penny—' she began. Her brow was furrowed in concern.

'What's wrong?' Surely she wasn't annoyed with me because I didn't come straight home after leaving the café?

'I tried to call you,' she continued.

'Did you not get my text? I just went for a walk after work. Sorry, I didn't mean to worry you.' I walked towards her but Mam remained stock-still on the doorstep, blocking my entrance.

'It's not that...' she whispered.

'Well, what is it then?' Her behaviour was starting to worry me. Had someone spotted Tadgh and me kissing in the dunes and already told Mam? You couldn't cough in this village without someone reporting it. If that was the reason for Mam's strange behaviour, I would have some explaining to do.

She looked around to make sure no one was listening, before pointing back into the house. 'Joe is here,' she hissed.

I fell back to reality with a bang. The time spent in the dunes with Tadgh felt like another world. Words were crashing around in my head: Joe, my husband, here. In Inishbeg Cove. Joe was here.

'He's here? In the house?' I managed. My first thought was for Lucy. I hadn't had time to prepare her. This was going to be confusing for her.

'He arrived about two hours ago,' she whispered. 'He's in the kitchen with your father and Lucy. The cheeky fecker is acting like nothing ever happened, but he won't fool me. Does he think we came down in the last shower?'

'Oh God.' My stomach lurched. 'How's Lucy been with him?'

'She was a bit shy at first, as you'd expect when she hasn't seen her father in *three months*.' Mam never missed an opportunity to get a dig in where Joe was concerned.

I took a deep breath and braced myself. For so long I had wanted Joe to do this. I had spent days praying for him to show me that he cared enough to follow us, but as the weeks had passed, I had given up all hope. Why now? Why today? It was almost as if he had a sixth sense, as if he knew I was about to leave him and start something new with Tadgh.

Mam stood to one side and I walked past her into the hallway. With a pounding heart, I made my way towards the kitchen. I knew I couldn't keep running forever. No matter what the future held for Joe and me, we had to talk. The time had arrived for us to decide where we went from here.

'Mama!' Lucy cried as soon as I appeared. I scooped her up.

'Ook, Dada came.' She pointed towards Joe, who was sitting at the table. Instantly I noticed that he had lost weight. His paunch was gone, and his face, which looked tired and drawn, was slimmer than I remembered, maybe because his beard was gone too. His eyes were red-rimmed and shadowed. He looked terrible. He was sipping a mug of coffee. I found myself cringing because it would have been made with instant granules instead of coffee beans, like he preferred. Then I reminded myself that instant coffee was the least of our problems. Dad was sitting opposite him, looking as if he wished he was anywhere else.

'Penny,' Dad said, standing up from the table. 'Well, I'll let ye two talk...' He excused himself and left so that it was just me, Lucy and Joe left in the kitchen together.

'I wasn't expecting you,' was all I could think of to say. 'Where's your car?'

'I was afraid that if I told you I was coming, you would refuse to see me,' he admitted sheepishly. 'I got the train to Limerick and then a taxi. You know I hate driving on those roads.'

Silence cloaked the air between us.

'So, how've you been?' he tried again.

'Honestly? It's been tough. Really tough.'

'I've missed you, Penny.' He stood up and came towards me. He moved to put his arms around me, but I put up a hand to stop him and he stepped back, looking suitably chastened.

'Come up here, Lucy, to see Daddy,' he tried to cajole her but she clung to me like a koala, burying her face in my neck.

He sat back down at the table.

'It took you long enough,' I said eventually.

'I'm sorry. My head has been all over the place.'

'And you think mine hasn't been?' I blazed.

Suddenly I became aware of Lucy looking at us. Her

small face was studying our expressions worriedly and I felt instantly contrite. I couldn't do this in front of her.

'Sit down for cup-a-tea, Mama,' Lucy ordered.

I took a seat across the table from Joe and let her pour me an imaginary cup from her teapot.

'She's got so big,' Joe said as we watched her play. 'Her speech – everything – she's grown up so much since I saw her.'

'She has,' I agreed. 'Three months is a long time when you're three.'

'I owe you an apology. I've treated you very badly, Penny. I know words can't make up for what I've done, but I need to try and explain. I've been in a bad place and, to be honest, I think I have been for a long time.'

Finally, I was getting an explanation. That was all I had wanted to hear for the last few months, but now that he was here in front of me, it all felt a bit ... strange. I was confused. Before he had arrived, I had been slowly starting to accept that my marriage was over, and I was emerging from the awful grief that came with that realisation. I had been starting to see the light, to feel more positive, but now every-thing had been thrown back up in the air and I didn't know how I was supposed to feel. I was angry, for sure, but mainly I felt hurt that it had taken Joe this long to decide that Lucy and I were what he wanted.

'I haven't been able to paint properly for months now,' he continued, 'and I stupidly believed that family life was stifling my painting, but when you and Lucy left, I was worse than ever. I realised that my creativity has been blocked for a long time. Since you've been gone, I haven't been able to eat, sleep or paint, and that's because I need you both. It was never you – it's always been me.'

I was stunned. Never had Joe opened up to me like this

before. He was admitting that *he* had the problem. How many times had I questioned myself, wondering if I was the reason for his difficult moods and ill temper? At times I had felt like I was going crazy, analysing everything I had said or done to make sense of his behaviour.

'I thought you had fallen out of love with me,' I admitted.

He shook his head. 'Oh Penny, it was never you – it was me. I've always loved you. I've been so consumed by my painting for my whole life, but art is meaningless without you.'

His ice-blue eyes locked on mine and I found I had to look away. Just an hour ago, I had been kissing another man. What had I been thinking? It now seemed as if a different person had melted into Tadgh's embrace, a different woman had felt her skin tingle, all her tiny hairs standing to attention, as Tadgh traced delicate kisses along the nape of her neck. No matter how frayed the ties of our marriage were, I was still Joe's wife.

'It hasn't felt like that for a while,' I said.

'When you left,' he continued, 'I thought I needed the space to figure my head out. I needed to see where the blockage was and to fix it. But after a few days alone, I realised that I was the problem.'

'But why didn't you come down here then?'

'When you were gone, I spiralled into an even darker place. I was drinking, trying to paint, then sabotaging whatever I did manage to paint, in a drunken stupor. It was like I had been possessed by demons.'

'But never mind about me – how could you stay away from Lucy for all that time?'

He shook his head. 'When I look back, I don't even recognise that man. I think I've had some kind of breakdown. I've been in a black place, Penny, but I'm slowly seeing the light.'

'We can't just take up where we left off, Joe. Everything has changed now.'

He nodded. 'I know that, but if you can forgive me, I will prove how much I adore you and Lucy. I will spend every day making it up to you both for the rest of my life.'

All I had wanted for so long was to hear him say these words, but now that he was standing before me saying them, I felt flat. Even if I managed to forgive him and we were able to move forward from here, I knew our marriage would be irreparably damaged. Like a vase that has been broken then glued back together, no matter how well it is repaired, you would still be able to see the cracks if you looked closely enough.

25

I had barely hung up when Greg came rushing in through the door of the post office. His ice-cream parlour was just up the street, but he must have dropped everything as soon as I had called.

'What's happened?' he said. His face was grey, and panic and worry threaded his voice.

I locked the door behind him so we wouldn't be disturbed.

'I'm cramping and bleeding.' I began to cry. Why had I let myself get my hopes up? Why had I thought I could have a happy-ever-after?

'Okay, we need to get you to the hospital,' he said calmly, taking charge of the situation. He was cool-headed and in control. I was glad I had him by my side when I was such a mess. He locked up the post office, guided me out to his car and we set off for Limerick. I placed my hands on my stomach and silently prayed for my babies to stay with me.

We barely spoke on the journey to the hospital; we were wrapped up in our own thoughts. The road hugged the wild Atlantic coastline where, beyond the window, the sun swept shadows like a cloak being pulled across the rolling green fields, and dairy cows grazed the luscious grass. Stone walls – painstakingly built by the bare hands of generations of farmers as they toiled to rid their land of rocks – cut seams through the landscape.

I was still in so much pain. Every few minutes I would be assaulted by a cramp so severe that I had to grip the dashboard until it passed.

'It'll be okay, Sarah,' Greg tried to reassure me after we had stopped in a gateway to let a tractor pass us on the narrow road. He reached across and gave my hand a squeeze.

I wasn't feeling so hopeful. Cramping and bleeding could only mean one thing. These babies were not meant to be.

Almost two hours later, we pulled into the hospital car park. After the long drive over the spine of the mountains and down the other side, I was glad to get out of the car to stretch my legs. My heart was hammering as we headed inside and towards the maternity unit.

We were greeted at the desk by a midwife who took my details before directing me to the emergency room. As we entered the waiting area, there were several other couples there, all waiting anxiously like us. Instantly I felt like a fraud; all around were women with large bumps. Some were even in early labour, but what about me? I had barely managed to make it past five and a half months.

Finally, my name was called.

'Sarah Klein?' a woman in blue hospital scrubs called out. It took me a moment to realise it was me they were referring to. I was still getting used to my married name.

Greg jumped up straight away. 'Come on, Sarah,' he said softly, holding my hand.

'My name is Sheila, I'm one of the emergency room doctors,' she said, shaking our hands. We followed her into a cubicle, where she directed me onto the bed. She asked me about my symptoms, and her expression gave nothing away as I described the vicious cramping and bleeding I had been experiencing. She spread the cool jelly on my stomach. Greg and I hardly dared to breathe as she began to scan me. I tried to make out the shapes of our babies on the screen, but it seemed to be a blur of black and white.

'Well, the good news is that I can hear two heartbeats,' she announced eventually. 'The fluid around the babies looks good too.'

Greg looked at me with incredulity and we looked back at the screen again.

'Here, would you like to listen to them?' she asked. Suddenly the room was filled with the welcome steady, thumping beat of our babies' hearts. It sounded like horses' hooves thundering over arid land. I looked at Greg, he looked at me, and we grinned.

'It would appear, though, that you have a low-lying placenta, which can often cause bleeding,' the doctor said. 'Usually the placenta will move up by itself later in the pregnancy.'

'Oh, thank God.' I exhaled in relief.

'So there is nothing wrong then?' Greg asked.

'The babies seem happy to me, but we'll do a CTG trace to check their heartrates, just to make sure everything is okay.'

She strapped two large elastic bands around me, attached to monitoring equipment, then she left us alone to watch the machine as it printed out a heartrate graph for both babies.

'What a relief.' Greg sighed heavily when we were alone again.

'I really thought we'd lost them.' I began to sob as the events of the day hit me. 'I got such a fright.'

'Hey,' Greg soothed, wiping my tears away. 'These babies are strong, like their mom – they're fighters.'

Sheila returned a short time later and examined the graphs. 'The traces are reassuring, which is good,' she said. 'Everything looks as it should be, so we'll let you go home. Make sure you keep an eye on the babies' movements and keep a record every day. If you notice a reduction or even if you're just unsure or feeling worried, come straight in to see us again. In the meantime, take it easy. Make sure you take lots of time to rest.'

Relief flooded over me. When we had come to the hospital a short time earlier, I thought my chance of motherhood had been snatched away from me, but leaving, still pregnant, felt indescribable. It felt like I had won the lottery not once but twice.

We both thanked the doctor profusely as we gathered up our things to leave.

'Come on, let's get you home,' Greg said, swinging his arm around my shoulders as we walked back out to the car park.

The next morning, I woke to find Lucy snoozing beside me. Her legs were draped across mine and she lay horizontally across the bed. Joe and I had stayed up talking into the early hours of the morning. He had been at pains to tell me that he was a changed man, and after only a few hours together I could see it was a more relaxed version of Joe who was sitting in my parents' kitchen.

Eventually we had called it a night. Joe had gone to sleep in the spare bedroom while I climbed in beside our daughter. I had folded her warm body into my arms as she snored gently, then spent several hours watching shadows creep around the edge of the window, my mind in a whir, until the sun began to rise on a new day.

I managed to extricate myself from Lucy's limbs, climbed out of bed and wrapped my dressing gown around me to stave off the chilly morning air. I went downstairs to the kitchen, to see Joe sitting at the table with a mug of coffee clasped in his hands.

'Morning, how did you sleep?' I asked.

'Great – best night I've had in a long time. It must be the sea air. What about you?'

'Not great,' I admitted.

He jumped up. 'Let me make you a coffee.' He boiled the kettle and began opening cupboard doors to locate the jar. He took down a mug and began to spoon the granules into it. I was waiting for him to make an annoying remark about how much he detested instant coffee, but it never came.

'It's a beautiful day out there,' he said, looking beyond the window at the clear blue sky. We should take Lucy down to the cove later.' He paused. 'I mean, if you'd like to, of course?' He placed the mug of coffee on the table in front of me and added a dash of milk, exactly the way I liked it.

'Good idea,' I said, embracing the warmth of the mug between my palms. 'She loves the beach.'

After Lucy woke, Mam, Dad, Joe and I sat around the table eating breakfast. The conversation was stilted, not helped by the fact that Mam was pointedly giving Joe a frosty reception. I was thankful for Lucy's chit-chat, which gave us all something to focus on.

After breakfast we left the cottage and crossed the road. The sea was like a viridian blanket stretching endlessly before us. Sunlight glistened off the water, giving it a metallic sheen. We strolled along by the sea wall until we reached the path leading down to the cove.

'I'd forgotten how beautiful this place is,' Joe said as we walked through the dunes. I was taken aback; I had never heard him compliment the village before. A few months after we had got together, I had been excited to bring him back home to see the village where I had grown up. I had thought that, as an artist, he would appreciate the dramatic landscapes, the vibrant colours of moss green and ochre under the gunpowder-blue sky on a stormy day, or the way the light shimmered off the water. I had expected him to be filled with inspiration after our weekend but to my disappointment, he had acted as though he could have been anywhere. Over the years, I had always thought him immune to the village's charms.

Once we had reached the sand, Lucy threw off her sandals and ran barefoot towards the water. I looked across at Joe, and saw the sheer joy in his eyes as he witnessed Lucy's love of the cove. We followed her down to the water's edge, where white-capped waves rolled forward and broke with a hiss at our feet.

Joe and I sat on a barnacle-studded rock while Lucy went around, poking sticks into rock pools. As the wind rippled the grass in the dunes above the cove, I couldn't help thinking that it had only been yesterday that Tadgh and I had hidden there as we shared a kiss. How quickly life could change tack and alter course. I felt myself blush as I thought about it.

'She's perfection, isn't she?' Joe said, breaking me out of my thoughts. We watched as Lucy toddled around, her curls peeking out from beneath her bonny sunhat.

'She sure is.'

Suddenly he turned towards me, his face creased with an intensity he usually reserved for his art. 'I can never be apart from either of you again.' He reached over for my hand, and I felt my resolve weaken as I let him take it in his own. Hadn't we both made mistakes? I was no angel either – I had kissed my ex-boyfriend, for God's sake. Didn't I owe it to my marriage and to our child to try again?

'I have to go get ready for work or I'll be late,' I said after a while, glancing at my watch and standing up.

'Work?'

I had forgotten that this would be news to Joe. It felt like so much had changed in the months we had been apart.

'I've been working part-time in Ruairí's café for the last few weeks.' I felt embarrassed admitting it to him. I was sure he would scorn the idea of his wife wiping down tables in a café. He would never understand me taking a job that involved no artistic endeavour. Then I felt annoyed with myself. What did it matter what he thought? If the last few months had taught me anything, it was that I was my own person and I couldn't let Joe's personality overshadow me any longer. I enjoyed working there, and that was all that mattered.

'But why are you working? I've never left you short of money.' He almost seemed offended, as if my having a job reflected poorly on him.

'It's not about the money. I enjoy it.'

'I guess I'm not the only one who's changed over the last few months,' he said, looking at me with a new admiration. It was as if he was seeing me properly for the first time. He stood up beside me and put his arm around my shoulder, and we began to walk towards Lucy. It was the most affection he had shown me in months, but it felt strange now, as if his arm belonged to a stranger instead of my husband. I wasn't able to let go and just enjoy the moment.

When we reached Lucy, he bent to help her strap on her sandals, then we headed back towards the dunes. She reached up for my hand and then for Joe's, and we strolled along in a trio, Lucy swinging between us. I liked how it felt; I had always looked at other families doing simple things like this with pang of regret, because my family wa so different to theirs but as the three of us walked together, I finally felt like we were one of them. The togetherness that

Joe, Lucy and I were experiencing right now was all I had ever wanted.

We were almost at the top of the path when suddenly Tadgh appeared, walking towards us. He had his surfboard tucked under his arm and was wearing his wetsuit like a second skin. His curly hair had been tossed around by the breeze and looked even wilder than normal. It felt as though a stone was sitting in my stomach and my heart began to pound like the wings of a bird trapped inside a cage.

'Hi, Tadgh,' Lucy greeted him in a sing-song voice.

'Hi there, Lucy.'

'Ook, Daddy came back.' She turned and pointed to Joe and me. I watched Tadgh's face change as Lucy's words registered. Our eyes met. There was an unmistakable gleam of hurt lurking in them. I found myself looking away. How the hell was I supposed to explain this to him? I prayed he wouldn't say anything to Joe about what had happened in the dunes the previous day.

'Tadgh, this is Joe, Joe, this is Tadgh,' I said, feeling flustered as I introduced them.

'Not many waves for surfing,' Joe remarked, stepping to the side to let Tadgh go past us.

'I'm paddling out to catch crabs, so the weather is perfect, actually.'

'What do you do with the crabs?' Joe asked, clearly intrigued.

'Well, I run the restaurant above you there set into the cliff,' Tadgh said, pointing towards it.

'Imagine, Penny,' Joe said, turning to me, 'in all the years I've been coming to this village, you've never taken me there! Well, hopefully we'll get there soon, Tadgh, and I'll get to sample some of those crabs.'

'Sure,' Tadgh said. 'I might see you there some time.' His

eyes flashed with anger as he passed me, and I longed to be able to run after him and explain it all. What must he think of me? Just hours ago, we had been wrapped in each other's arms, and now here I was, reunited with my husband and playing happy families once again.

'Do you know something, Penny?' Joe said, oblivious to my turmoil, as we walked back to the cottage.

'What?'

'I think that being in this village even for a day has given me so much clarity. The fresh air, the landscapes, the absence of all the hustle and bustle that is our life in Dublin – my head feels so much better for it.'

'Well, I've always said this village has magical qualities.'

He nodded. 'Instead of rushing back to Dublin, I think we should stay for a bit longer.'

His words brought me back to reality. Had Joe really thought that, as soon as he arrived, we'd all pile into the car and go on our merry way back to Dublin, reunited as a family once again? Surely not. I knew we needed to work on our marriage, but I still didn't know what the future held for us. So much hurt had been concreted between the fractures that it was going to take an awful lot of time and labour to chisel it away again. And even if we did succeed, would we be able to rebuild our relationship again on a solid foundation or would we just be left with the fragments of a shattered marriage?

SARAH

When I woke the next morning, I realised that I had slept right through my alarm. As soon as I climbed into bed the night before, the emotional toll of the day had caught up on me and I had fallen into the soundest sleep.

I opened my eyes and checked the clock on my bedside locker and realised that the post office was due to open in fifteen minutes. I rolled over as fast as I could onto my side, then put my feet on the floor before attempting to stand up. It was the only way I could get out of bed lately without Greg's help. I dressed as quickly as I could and headed downstairs to the kitchen, my hairbrush in my hand. Greg was already downstairs eating breakfast.

'Why didn't you wake me?' I asked when I reached the bottom of the stairs.

'I thought you could use the sleep,' he said, biting into a slice of buttered toast. 'How are you feeling?'

'I'm fine,' I said, reefing the hairbrush through my hair. 'But I'm going to be late – I meant to open up in ten minutes.'

"You're not seriously thinking of going to work, are you?'

'Of course I am! Who else will do it?'

'Don't worry. I've arranged for Maureen to cover for you to give you a chance to rest.'

I couldn't believe what I was hearing. 'Greg, you can't do that! You should have checked with me first.'

'But Maureen doesn't mind. She's delighted to be able to help out.'

'I know that, and I appreciate it, I really do, but I can't expect Maureen to work there – she's busy enough with the B&B.'

'She doesn't mind.' He looked abashed. 'I thought I was doing you a favour.'

'But I still have to go to work, Greg. The villagers need their post office.'

'But the doctor said you've to rest!'

'Honestly, Greg, you're overreacting. What difference will it make if I sit in the post office or sit at home? I promise you that I'll take it easy.'

'Well, I was thinking about that...' He put his toast on his plate. 'Maybe you should look into hiring someone to give you a hand. You're going to need help to cover your maternity leave after the babies are born, anyway. At least if you hire them now, it'll give you loads of time to get them trained up.'

'But I can't afford to – the post office barely pays *me* a wage. I've been putting a little bit aside each week so that I'll have the money to pay someone to cover me for the six months of my maternity leave, but I can't afford to extend it. I couldn't afford to hire anyone even if I wanted to,' I added.

'It's only for a few months, until the babies are out of danger. I'm sure we'll be able to survive on my wage for a little while. My business is getting busier; I'm getting new restaurants placing orders with me every month. I know it'll be tight, especially with two new mouths to feed, but it'll be worth it.'

'It's not even just the money, Greg, I *like* my job, I like meeting people. I'm not due for a few months yet. I'll go stir crazy sitting in the house all day by myself. I'm better off in work.'

'But won't it be worth it if it keeps the babies safe?'

'Greg, that's emotional blackmail! Of course I want the best outcome for our twins and I would never knowingly put them at risk, but I also think sitting working in the post office isn't jeopardising them. I'll do exactly what the hospital told me to do and keep track of their movements. I promise you I won't take any chances.'

'I'd rather you just rested now until they're born. It's not worth taking any risks – why can't you see that?'

'Well, you can't lock me up, Greg,' I said reaching for my bag. 'Now, if you'll excuse me, I'm going to work.'

'P enny for them?' Ruairí said over the din of the coffee machine as it spurted out frothed milk.

'What?' I asked, turning around. Apart from the racket that the coffee machine was making, the café was unusually quiet. Autumn was starting to push in now and the leaves were showing the first hints of amber among the green, hinting that the end of summer was here.

Over the last few days I had noticed a big drop in customers now that the warm days of summer were coming to an end and holidaying families were beginning to head home in preparation for sending their children back to school. There had been a considerable drop in temperature too. Bare arms were now covered by sweaters and jackets, and shorts had been packed away for another year. The end of the summer was a watershed moment in Inishbeg Cove. It always felt as though the village was being handed back to the locals to tend for the winter months. It was a chance for its people to catch their breath after a hectic summer. And with Joe's arrival in the village, I too felt like I had arrived at a watershed moment in my life.

'Your thoughts – you know, penny for them?' he repeated.

'Oh, sorry,' I said. 'I was miles away.'

'Clearly.' He swung the tea towel he was carrying over his shoulder. 'What's the matter? You've been away with the fairies all day.'

I put down the steel milk jug and turned to face him, resting my back against the cool marble of the countertop. 'You'll never guess who turned up at Mam and Dad's yesterday.'

His eyes widened with disbelief. 'Not Joe?' he said, shaking his head.

I nodded.

'Well, that's a good thing, isn't it?'

'Yeah...'

'But?'

'Well...' I hesitated.

'What? I thought that was what you wanted.'

I sighed. 'It was. I mean, it is, but ... I don't know. I just thought I'd feel different. For so long, what I wanted most in the world was for him to follow us here, but now that he has ... I feel ... well ... a bit deflated, to be honest.'

'Well, that's only natural. You've spent a long time apart. It'll take a while to get things back on track between you, but at least he wants to try again. You were so worried that your marriage was over.'

'I guess I've realised that in the time we've been apart, so much has changed. I've changed!'

'And has he changed?'

I paused to consider Ruairí's words. 'He says so, and I think he has.'

'So can't you both forgive and forget?'

'It's not that simple.'

'It can be if you want it to be, Penny.'

I shook my head. 'I wasn't expecting to feel quite so angry with him. I think he expects we'll just take up where we left off now that he's here, but I don't know if things can ever be the same between us again.' I exhaled heavily. 'I'm so confused, Ruairí.'

Ruairí folded his arms across his chest and gave me a sideways smile. 'Would this be something to do with a certain person by the name of Tadgh?'

'Of course not!'

'Come on, Penny, you can be honest with me.'

'Well, maybe just a bit...' I admitted, feeling my face flush at the mention of his name.

'Aha! I knew it!' he exclaimed triumphantly. 'And what about you? What do you want, Penny?'

'That's the thing. I just don't know. Last week I would have said having my little family back together was the thing I wanted most in the world, but this week I'm not sure. I have so many worries, like what if he does this to me again?'

'There are no guarantees in life. If you do want to give your marriage another shot, then you have to trust that it'll all work out the way it's supposed to.'

'I don't know what to do. I feel I owe it to my marriage to try again – especially for Lucy's sake. I just wish someone would tell me the right thing to do.'

'There's no right or wrong in love. You have to follow your heart and put your trust in it to lead you along the right path.'

'You're right.' I sighed and glanced at my watch. It was a quarter past two. 'I'd better go. Mam will probably be putting Joe through the third degree.' I leant forward and planted a kiss on his cheek. 'Thank you, Ruairí.'

'For what?' He was taken aback.

'For listening to me. You've been such a good friend to me since I came home.'

Ruairí blushed. I left him alone and went into the kitchen to grab my jacket and bag.

'Will I see you tomorrow?' he asked, handing me a loaf of still-warm Guinness bread.

'As long as you still need me and I'm here in the village, I'm all yours. And when I go back to Dublin, I won't leave you in the lurch. I'll give you plenty of notice.'

'Don't worry about me, I'll be fine. You have to look after yourself.'

'See you tomorrow then,' I called and stepped outside the door, carrying the paper bag containing the bread, my mind in a whirl. I breathed in the salty air, pulling it deeply into my lungs, and suddenly collided with something hard.

'Oh God, sorry!' I said. I stepped back, startled when I realised it was Tadgh.

'I thought you'd already be finished,' he mumbled.

'I got held up...'

He had obviously been trying to avoid me by leaving it later to get his coffee. He nodded and went to move around me to go into the café.

'Tadgh – wait. I need to explain—'

'No, you don't, it's okay,' he said.

'Please, hear me out. Joe just turned up without telling me. I had no idea he was coming. I'm so sorry.'

He pursed his lips, nodding. 'Hey, you need to prioritise your family, you've a child together. I get that.'

I nodded. A silence fell over us like a cloak, leaving us standing there awkwardly under its weight. There was nothing left to say.

'Well, I'd better get on,' Tadgh said, pushing open the

café door before pausing and turning back to face me. 'Look, if I don't see you before you go back to Dublin, then I hope it all works out for you, Penny. I really do. I hope you and Joe will be very happy together.' Then he walked into the café – and out of my life for the second time.

29

SARAH

Tears pricked at my eyes as I made my way down the path from my cottage towards the post office. I immediately regretted snapping at Greg as soon as I had stepped outside the door. As I looked out at the sea, it matched my mood with its wild and raging roar. The wind whipped my hair around my face and rang in my ears. Greg and I rarely fought, and I hated it when we were on bad terms with one another. Of course we had disagreed over things in the past, like every couple does, but they had been minor things, like when I wanted to paint our bedroom marshmallow pink and Greg had overruled me. In the end, we had laughed about it. We shared the same views and outlook on the big things – the stuff that really mattered. Except for now. It felt as though I was sitting on the deck of a boat in a stormy sea; my whole world was titled at a funny angle and I didn't like it. I just wanted us to be on the level again, the way we usually were.

I was feeling smothered. Greg wanted to wrap me up in cotton wool, but I had always worked in the post office. It was all I had ever known. Although I was really excited to be a mother, I also didn't want to lose my identity. I loved how the villagers relied on me to do their daily business or even just to come in for a chat. Either way, they were treasured customers. The truth was, no matter how much the villagers needed their post office, I needed them just as much.

As I sorted through the mail sacks that morning, I still hoped that Greg would drop by the post office, as he usually did, at one o'clock so we could head into Ruairí's for lunch together, but when the minute hand showed quarter past, then half past, and he still hadn't arrived, I knew he wasn't coming. I was so deflated. It seemed we were both entrenched in our views. I really thought that once he'd had some time to think about it, he would come around to my way of thinking. The hardest part was that I knew he wanted the best for our babies, just like I did, so it was hard to accept that we had such different opinions. And I wasn't sure how we could compromise. Our relationship had been such a whirlwind, and it was now being tested for the first time.

'Hello, Mrs Manning,' I said, when she came in on her daily visit. She usually dropped me in a few eggs laid by her hens, but more often than not it was just for a chat. 'It's a wild day out there, isn't it?' I did my best to try to sound cheery. She had full make-up on as usual: blue eyeshadow brightened her eyes and ruby-red lipstick coloured her lips. She looked as glamorous as always with her scarlet-red hair set in soft curls around her face.

'Well, I'm still here and that's a bonus at my age.' She chuckled. As she got nearer to the counter, she narrowed her eyes. 'What's wrong with you, love?' she asked. 'You look like you could go ten rounds with Mike Tyson and win.'

I could never hide anything from her. She knew me too well. Maybe it was because it was Mrs Manning, or maybe it was her choice of words, but the tears started then and I couldn't stop them.

'Heavens above! Let me in there to you this minute,' the older lady ordered.

I opened the security door to let her come in behind the counter. She shuffled in and when she reached me, she steadied herself before taking me in her arms. 'What is it, my dear? It's not the babies, is it?'

I shook my head.

'Is it Greg? I hope nothing's wrong.'

I told her about our trip to the hospital the previous day and explained how Greg wanted me to stop working.

'But the doctor said I can keep working for now if I take it easy,' I added.

'Oh dear, I'm sorry. You will work it out,' she counselled. 'He's just worried about you, Sarah. You know he's doing it with a good heart.'

'You're right.' I sighed, wiping tears away with the back of my hand.

'He means well, Sarah – he just wants to take care of you. But I also know how independent you are, and how important the post office is to you.'

'I'm practically sitting down all day and I've stopped lifting anything heavy – I just don't see what difference it makes whether I'm sitting in the post office or at home.'

'I guess he's worried about the effect stress could have on the babies.'

'Come on, Mrs Manning, running the post office is hardly stressful. If the queue is more than three people long, that's about as stressful as it gets. I just wish he'd see that arguing over it is causing me far more stress than going to work does.'

Mrs Manning nodded. 'You still have a while to go yet, so

unless your doctors have advised you to stop working then surely Greg can see he's being a little over-protective?'

'That's not how he sees it,' I said.

'Greg is a reasonable man; do you want me to have a word with him?'

I shook my head. 'Thanks, but I think we need to sort this out ourselves.'

'I think that's probably wise, my dear.'

THAT NIGHT I lay in bed as Greg snored softly beside me. We hadn't spoken as we ate the dinner he had cooked, and we had gone to bed without speaking.

He let out a loud snore and turned over in bed. I wondered how he was even able to sleep when my mind was so full of worry. I sighed, pulled up my pyjama top and placed my hands on my ballooning abdomen. I could feel our babies turn and twist beneath my hands, their angular arms and legs jutting out of me. They really were a miracle. *Our* miracle. I just wished we could both enjoy this special time instead of ruining it by arguing. For the first time in our lives we were not on the same page – we weren't even on the same chapter.

'Mama!' Lucy cried, jumping off the swing that Mam and Dad had recently bought for their back garden and running into my arms.

'How's my gorgeous girl?' I lifted her up.

'Did Ruairí give me a cake?' she asked, her blue eyes round with excitement. She adored the treats he sent home for her every day, and would jump up and down with anticipation when I came through the door. Sometimes I wondered if she was happier to see me or the cake.

'He sure did,' I said. 'How does chocolate biscuit cake sound?'

She squeezed her pudgy arms around my neck. 'Yummy!'

I sat her on my hip and carried her into the house. Joe and Dad were sitting at the kitchen table and Mam stood washing dishes at the sink.

'There you are, Penny,' Joe said as I came through the door. He stood up, came over and kissed my cheek. I instantly felt self-conscious in front of my parents. It was the most intimate we had been in months, and I felt myself stiffen at his touch. 'How was work?'

'Busy,' I replied.

'Sit down, *a ghrá*, and take the weight off your feet,' Dad said, pulling out a chair for me. I flopped down into it and Lucy sat on her grandad's knee.

'Well, I have some news that might cheer you up,' Joe said. 'Oh yeah?'

'I'm after getting the Henley commission!' He beamed. 'I was just telling your parents about it before you came home.'

The Henley commission was for a retiring bank CEO. Joe had pitched for the job months back and it was worth a lot of money.

'That's great, Joe,' I said doing my best to feign enthusiasm. Although I knew he had been after this commission for months, I couldn't help feeling deflated by his news. He had professed to have changed but, judging by his exuberant mood today, his form was still clearly being dictated by his artistic achievements. He was always in a good mood when life was going well for him, but how would he react when things started to go wrong – which they would? What would happen when the bad times came, if he got another bad review or if he lost out on a commission? Would we all have to suffer? My biggest fear was that, if we returned to Dublin, he might switch straight back to being moody, erratic Joe.

'And the good news is, your parents have kindly offered to mind Lucy for us this evening,' he continued, grinning across the table at me. 'I thought we might head up to that restaurant up on the cliffs to celebrate ... what was the guy's name again?'

'You mean Tadgh's place?' I felt my stomach constrict.

'That's the one.'

I watched Mam as she turned around from the sink, out of sight of Joe, and raised her eyebrows at me. I knew what she was thinking. Was I really going to bring my husband to my ex-boyfriend's restaurant – an ex-boyfriend who I had grown close to over the last few weeks? I looked away from her.

'Actually, Joe, I'm exhausted,' I lied.

'Oh, come on, Penny, it'll do us good to have some alone time. It'll give us a chance to talk properly. And I want to check out that restaurant before we head back to Dublin. Apparently, the guy turned down the chance to get a Michelin star – isn't that crazy? We'll be leaving Inishbeg Cove soon, and who knows when I'll be back down again.'

Joe and I still hadn't discussed our return to Dublin, or even when it might happen. I had deliberately changed the subject whenever he raised it, but it seemed he had made the decision for both of us.

'Honestly, I'm happy you got the commission, but all I want to do is crash out on the sofa. I was run off my feet all afternoon. I'm going to shower and get changed,' I said standing up and going down to the bedroom.

'You poor thing, Penny,' Joe said, following me. 'I know you're tired but honestly, I don't understand why you are working there.' He shook his head and splayed his hands out in the air, as if it was all too perplexing. 'If it's too much, you can give it up.'

'I told you, I like it there.' I bristled.

'Anyway, what do you say?' He sat down on the side of the bed.

'Maybe another time.'

'I thought you said it was the best restaurant around

here. Anyone would think you don't want me to go there,' he added.

'Of course I want to take you there...' I found myself agreeing. Joe was sharp and I was worried that if I made any more excuses, he would start to grow suspicious. 'Look, just let me freshen up. I'm sure I'll feel better after I shower.'

'IT'S A QUAINT LITTLE PLACE, isn't it?' Joe said as we entered the arched stone doorway and stepped into the cavern carved out of the rock, created by the sea over thousands of years.

I knew it was silly, but I couldn't help feeling a tinge of defensiveness. 'It's probably the most unique restaurant in Ireland.'

We walked up to the front desk. Tadgh was bending over, explaining something on the menu to a couple at a nearby table. My heart rate quickened. What was I going to say to him? What would he think? He hadn't seen us come in, which gave me a few seconds to study his broad physique before he noticed me. His angular jawline was dotted with dark stubble and he smiled easily as he chatted. I watched as he straightened up and saw us. His cool blue eyes met mine. I immediately felt heat creep into my cheeks as the smile left his face. I prayed Joe wouldn't notice.

'Penny, Joe, you made it!' he said as he finally snapped back into restaurateur mode. He came towards us and put his hand out to shake Joe's.

Joe clasped Tadgh's hand and pumped it. 'She finally brought me.' He laughed.

'Well, let me show you to a table.'

We followed Tadgh through the candle-lit chambers

until we came to a stop beside a table in the middle of the restaurant. 'Is this okay?'

'It's perfect,' I said.

'Actually, it might be a bit noisy,' Joe said, looking around at the other customers. 'Have you anywhere quieter?'

Inwardly, I cringed.

'Sure,' Tadgh said. We followed him to the back of the cavern, to a table tucked into an alcove at one side of the cave. 'How about here?'

'What do you think, Penny?' Joe asked me.

'It's good with me.'

'If the lady is happy, then I am too,' Joe said, winking at Tadgh as if it was a man-to-man joke. Tadgh indulged him with a smile, but it didn't quite stretch up to his eyes.

'Now, here are your menus. Everything is available except for the hake; we ran out earlier. And the catch of the day is monkfish.'

Then he left us alone to study the menus.

'Hmm, this looks good,' Joe said in approval as he read through it. 'Let me guess, Penny, you're going to order the prawns, aren't you?'

'Well...'

Joe slapped the table in victory. 'I know you too well.' He laughed.

'I guess I'm a creature of habit,' I admitted.

Tadgh returned a few minutes later and took our orders. Joe ordered the crab claws while I went with my predictable prawn dish.

'And any wine for you both?' Tadgh asked.

'Yes, actually, can we order a bottle of Sancerre too?' Joe looked at me. 'That's okay with you, isn't it, Penny?' he asked as an afterthought.

'Sure,' I agreed. Tadgh wrote it down in his flip-top notebook.

'So, how long have you known Tadgh?' Joe asked as Tadgh retreated towards the kitchen.

'We were in school together,' I said.

'Ooh, an old school pal! I wonder if he has any naughty tales about you.'

'Don't be silly!' I spluttered. 'Anyway, how did you and Lucy get on in the playground earlier?' I asked, trying to steer the conversation back to the safer territory that was our daughter.

'It was very funny, actually. There was a little boy there and the two of them hit it off. When it was time for us to go home, she ran over and gave him a kiss.'

I laughed as Joe recounted Lucy's escapades. Soft candlelight flickered shadows around the walls and the low buzz of chatter echoed under the vaulted ceiling. Under different circumstances, it would have been such a romantic setting.

'You know, I think playschool will be really good for her,' Joe continued.

I nodded, feeling the familiar churn in my stomach that I always felt whenever Joe mentioned returning to Dublin. Something had changed. I wasn't sure what, but recently thoughts of my old life made me feel claustrophobic.

'Now then, the crab claws and the prawns,' Tadgh said, placing our plates in front of us a short time later.

'Thank you,' Joe replied.

'It looks delicious, Tadgh,' I mumbled.

'Well, *bon appetit*,' Tadgh said, leaving us alone once more.

'Actually, can I have some black pepper?' Joe called after him.

'Sure.' Tadgh returned with the canister moments later and started grinding it over Joe's plate.

'Penny tells me you were in school together,' Joe said to Tadgh when he had finished, and I thought I was going to be sick. 'So, tell me, what was my wife like as a teenager? I've a feeling she was a bit of a wild child.'

I winced and couldn't bear to look at Tadgh's face.

'I can assure you that Penny has always been a lady,' Tadgh replied tactfully. I felt myself start to breathe again. I was so relieved that he had the sense not to mention our relationship. 'I'd better go,' he said, nodding towards a man who had just entered the restaurant and was waiting at the front desk to be seated. 'Enjoy your food.'

As we tucked into our food, Joe continued to chat away, but I was wrapped in the blanket of my thoughts. Every now and again I would catch Tadgh's eye and I was sure I could see flashes of irritation burning in their moody depths.

'Sorry, what?' I asked. Joe's words had pulled me out of the rabbit hole of my own head.

'I don't think you're listening to a word I'm saying, Penny!' Joe said impatiently. 'I was thinking, we should probably head back to Dublin tomorrow. What do you reckon?'

'Tomorrow?' I repeated, almost choking on my food.

'Well, why not? It's time we got back to normal.'

I swallowed. I didn't feel ready yet. It seemed Joe wanted us to slot straight back into our old lives as if nothing had happened but, I had changed since I had been away.

'I can't leave Ruairí in the lurch,' I said.

'Come on, Penny, I'm sure he doesn't expect you to give him a month's notice. The Ts&Cs on your contract can't be *too* legally binding.' He laughed at his own joke.

I couldn't help feeling irked. 'I know we don't have a

formal arrangement, but Ruairí is a friend and I want to be fair.'

'Well, we need to go soon. September isn't far away. Lucy is due to start playschool, and I have that commission to start now as well.'

'I'll talk to Ruairí tomorrow and see what he says,' I said to appease him. I knew Ruairí wouldn't have a problem with me leaving, especially now the busy summer season was over for another year, but *I* needed more time. I couldn't delay my return to Dublin indefinitely, but the village had been a safe haven for me during the stormiest time in my life. It had helped to heal my wounded soul over the last few months, and I wasn't ready to say goodbye.

31

PENNY

I watched the fisherman as he stood on his boat, turned his face up to the salt-scented air, and took a sniff. I could remember asking Dad, when I was a child, what they were doing, and he had explained that they were checking to see if a storm was coming. After spending years on fishing boats, their nostrils had become finely tuned to detect a change in the weather and, despite all the technological advances in shipping forecasts and storm warnings, it seemed the older fishermen still preferred to rely on their senses.

The petrol-blue ocean before me was wild and energetic. The tide was in almost as far as the sleek black rocks, and the waves crashed against the sea wall, unleashing their pent-up ferocity. A jet of sea spray suddenly arced over the wall and I quickly stepped back to avoid being soaked.

I was on my way to the café. Just as the change in the air signalled that summer was drawing to a close, so too was life in the village for me. I couldn't shake off a heavy sense of foreboding. A feeling of impending dread had settled over me in recent days. I knew my days working in the café were numbered. I had managed to fob Joe off by telling him that Ruairí needed me to stay on for another week to see off the last of the holidaymakers, but I couldn't prolong our return to Dublin forever. Our departure was inevitable. Even Mam and Dad seemed to have accepted that we would be leaving soon.

I tried telling myself that this was what I wanted. My old life had been great. We lived in a lovely part of Dublin, where beautiful terraces of Georgian red-bricks fronted pretty parks, safe for children to play in. We had myriad cafés, bars and bijou restaurants on our doorstep. There was every convenience, from upmarket hair salons to artisan delis. There were theatres and galleries and quirky antique markets – all things I had once thought important, yet which I hadn't missed a bit since I had been back in the village. The thing was, before I returned to Inishbeg Cove, I had been happy with my Dublin life. I knew that once I'd had the chance to settle back in, I would like it again. I was sure of it.

To give Joe his due, he was making an effort. Although his moods were still heavily influenced by his art, I felt that he no longer saw me simply as an accessory to his life. My absence had tipped the scales a little more in my favour, and things felt more balanced between us. I really believed he was trying harder to be a better husband.

In the distance, I could see a black shape emerging from the white water. Only a lunatic would go into the water in this weather, I thought. It was probably an adrenaline-seeking surfer chasing the ultimate wave. I watched the figure for a moment and realised, as they came closer to the shore, that it was Tadgh. Surely he wasn't fishing for crabs in this weather? He was positively mad. He knew the sea and the dangers it could pose. He had lived in this village long enough to know what it could do if you didn't respect it. The sea could be cruel, and could turn on you faster than you could take a breath.

I waited until he had emerged from the foam and tucked his board underneath his arm. I saw that he hadn't caught any crabs. Surely he hadn't just gone out to surf? Even though every synapse within me told me to walk away, my feet wouldn't move. I stood rooted to the spot, as if I had no control over my own legs. It was as though I was drawn to him by a magnetic force. I waited as he climbed the path from the cove back up towards the village.

'Penny?' He looked taken aback to see me when he reached the top. He ran a hand through his dark, wavy hair, sleeking it back off his face. God, he looked so good.

'Have you got a death wish? Surely you would give the surf a miss on a day like today?' I was angry at his cavalier attitude to the elements.

'Best kind of day for it if you want to clear your head.'

'If you say so...'

'I hope you and Joe enjoyed your meal the other day?'

'I'm sorry about that.'

'For what?'

'It wasn't my idea. I know it was awkward, and I really didn't want to bring my husband to my ex-boyfriend's restaurant, but he really wanted to try it out and—'

'That was all a long time ago, Penny,' he said. 'And you're free to eat wherever you want.' He shrugged, seemingly blasé about the whole thing.

I was making a fool of myself. He didn't seem to be in the least bit bothered. Maybe I was blowing this out of all proportion. Had I really seen pain lurking in his eyes in the restaurant that day? Maybe it had been wishful thinking on my part...

'Okay, I'll let you at it,' I said, turning and walking in the direction of the café, feeling mortification burn through my body with every step.

'Penny, wait—' he called after me.

I turned around to face him.

'I'm sorry,' he said, shaking his head. 'I didn't mean that. I know it was awkward ... for both of us.'

I nodded, feeling a strange sense of relief that it hadn't just been me. That he had felt it too.

'So, how's everything with you and Joe?' he asked.

I cringed. How was I supposed to answer that question? 'We're working it out.'

'So, I guess you'll be leaving to go back to Dublin soon?'

'Well, Joe wants to...'

'And you?'

'Yeah, I do too. Although the summer here has been lovely, I'm looking forward to getting on with my life again. And Lucy is due to start playschool, so it'll be a new start for us all.'

'That's good. I'm happy for you.'

'Yeah.' I tried to sound brighter than I felt.

'You don't look too happy.'

'I guess I feel a bit ... strange. Spending the summer in the village has been lovely. I'd forgotten how special this place is. I never thought I'd say this, but I'm going to miss it. But I guess I can't put it off forever...'

'Sometimes a little recharge is almost as good as a fresh start.'

I nodded, feeling my heart swell. He was being so understanding of my situation. 'But I think that spending time in the village again has changed me … I can't explain it.'

'I think I can…'

'What do you mean?'

'I think that having some time and space to think has allowed the old Penny to emerge.'

I smarted. 'I'm still me, Tadgh.' The wind seemed to sweep the words out of my mouth, and I instantly regretted being so defensive.

'You know that's not what I'm saying. I just meant you've changed over the summer. I hardly recognised you when we met on the beach that morning – you were so different from how I remembered you as a teenager, but over the last few months I've watched you slowly come back to the girl I remember.'

I couldn't help smiling.

'When we kissed that day…' he continued.

'Please—' I said, putting up my hand to stop him. 'I should never have done that.' I had been feeling increasingly guilty over the last few days about betraying Joe. How had I been unfaithful to my husband? Surely, despite all Joe's faults, he didn't deserve that? The shame was something I would have to live with forever.

'You can't deny there's still something between us – there always has been, Penny.'

I felt my heart beat a little faster. Suddenly the roar of the sea seemed to fade into the background, as if someone had turned down a volume dial.

'Maybe you're right,' I said carefully, 'but I'm still married, and I need to give my marriage another shot.' I needed to be loyal to Joe. I paused before adding, 'I-I love Joe.'

His gaze shifted out across the steel-grey horizon as he

nodded. 'Then I wish you the best of luck. I really do. You might not believe me, but I only want you to be happy.'

'Thanks,' I said. 'I really appreciate that.'

We stood awkwardly for a few moments, letting the roar of the sea fill the silence left behind by our words. Everything had already been said.

I turned the key in the lock of the post office door, ready to close up for another day. I began walking home towards the cottage but, rather than going straight there, I found myself crossing over to walk along the cove to clear my head.

Since we had had our big argument, not a word had passed between Greg and me. I hated every minute of the silence; the atmosphere in the house was awful. We had never gone to bed on an argument before, so this was uncharted territory. It seemed we both felt strongly that we were right, and I didn't know how we would ever reach a compromise.

The wind whistled in my ears as I walked through the dunes and eventually reached the smooth brown-sugar sand. The sea boiled and frothed, surging onto the beach with an angry hiss. A gull swooped low over the water before soaring upwards again in the sulky sky, trying to gain traction on the choppy wind.

When I reached the old smugglers' caves at the other end of the beach, I turned to come back. My legs were starting to tire, and I was feeling the weight of my bump with every step I took. Then I spotted Penny Murphy in the distance, sitting on the rocks and staring pensively out at the water. There was something about the way she sat perched there, that reminded me of one of the illustrations in a copy of *The Little Mermaid* my mother had bought me as a child. Although I didn't know Penny well, I could tell that something was bothering her.

'Hi, Penny,' I called as I got closer, my words barely audible above the wind.

She startled. Clearly, she had been lost in her own world.

'Hi, Sarah. Sorry – I was miles away,' she called back.

'Well, there's nowhere better than the cove if you need to do some thinking,' I said.

'You look out there and, no matter what's going on in your world, the ocean still washes in and out and the sun rises and sets above it every day.'

I stopped walking, sensing that perhaps there was more Penny needed to say. 'It certainly puts everything into perspective, doesn't it?' I agreed. 'What might seem important or big in our world right now is nothing in the grand scheme of life. We're only dots in the book of time. It's reassuring, in a way.'

'How are your babies doing?' she asked, nodding towards my bump.

'They're good.' I automatically placed my hands on my abdomen, as if to reassure myself that they were still in there. 'Obviously it's a bit risky at my age, but hopefully everything will go all right.' Automatically, I crossed my fingers behind my back, like I always did whenever I thought about the future and getting these babies here safely.

'They'll be with you before you know it,' Penny remarked.

'Well, hopefully not too soon,' I replied cautiously.

'Sorry, I didn't mean that—' she said quickly. 'Sometimes I don't think before I speak.'

'Don't be silly,' I said. 'I knew what you meant. Mind if I sit down? My back aches if I stand for too long these days.'

'Of course,' she said. I eased myself down onto a nearby rock.

'Oooh, that's better.' I sighed with relief. 'I think I saw your husband with your little girl in the playground yesterday.'

'Yeah, that would have been Joe.'

'Will you be staying on in the village for a while?'

She shook her head. 'We'll be heading back home to Dublin soon.'

'It'll be nice to get back home. I'm sure you're looking forward to it?'

Her gaze dropped and she looked out at the lead-grey water. 'Yeah. We have to get back to normal eventually, I guess.'

If she was looking forward to returning to Dublin, she certainly didn't show it. Her demeanour was lacklustre.

'As the saying goes, all good things must come to an end...' I replied.

'I have to say, I'll miss this place when I'm gone. It's funny – when I was younger and came home from college in Dublin at the weekends, I couldn't wait to get away again, but spending the summer here has really allowed me to see the village for the amazing place it is.'

'I think it's only when we get older that we truly appreciate things like where we came from, where we belong, our family and our roots.'

She nodded. 'You think you want something so badly, and you spend so long chasing after it, but then you get it and you realise it's not what you wanted at all.'

I sensed we were no longer talking about the village and had moved on to something deeper, although I was unsure what.

'Sometimes we might outgrow places or people, but never those that are worth having in our lives,' I replied.

'But how do you know if something is worth having in your life?' She turned and looked at me. Her eyes met mine, and in their grey-green depths I could see confusion. I guessed then that we were talking about her marriage. Although I didn't know anything about her relationship with her husband, the fact that she had been in the village alone with her daughter for the last three months and then he had showed up out of the blue led me to think that they were having difficulties. There was something about Penny – a vulnerability, if you like – and I thought she might need someone to talk to. I knew she was staying with her parents and she had become friendly with Ruairí in the café too, but sometimes it was easier to talk to a stranger: someone who could look in from the outside and could listen without any preconceived opinions or agendas.

'That's a big question,' I began. 'But I suppose when the good times you spend with that person outweigh the bad times, then it's worth fighting for. Even though you will disagree now and then, if you both know that ultimately you are on the same page, then that will get you through the difficult times.' I was deliberately being as vague in my response as she had been in her question. I could tell she wasn't ready to open up fully to me, but she obviously needed to talk. 'I always think that if you can have a laugh with someone, then you still have something special,' I added.

'I've seen you in the café with your husband – Greg, isn't it?' she said.

'That's himself.'

'I know I don't know you well, so I hope you don't mind me saying that you two always look very happy together.'

Her words made me pause. There was me thinking I was doling out the advice, but she was right. I had lost sight of that over the last few days. On the whole, Greg and I were good together. Although we might have hit a speed bump recently, I knew we could surmount it because our relationship was worth striving for. 'We are...' I began, 'but lookit, I'd be lying if I said we didn't have our ups and downs like every couple.' I felt I owed it to Penny to be honest and let her know that everyone had their problems, no matter how perfect their lives might look on the outside. 'Is everything okay, Penny? I ventured.

She smiled at me. 'Sorry, I'm sure you've better things to be doing than listening to me yakking on.'

'I don't know your situation so please don't take this the wrong way, but if it helps, I firmly believe that you only get one life and you have to live it without any regrets. Listen to your heart, and you can't go far wrong.'

'I think you're right,' she said, climbing down from her rock and standing on the sand, which was littered with bladderwrack. 'I'd better get home or Lucy will be wondering where I am.'

I went to stand too, although I had to use a nearby rock to lever myself up. 'If you ever need someone to talk to, you know where I am,' I said. 'I mean it. It's not all letters and stamps in the post office, you know – you'd be surprised at the number of people who come through my door just for a chat and cuppa.'

'Thanks for listening.'

'No bother. Now, I'd better head on too.' Talking to Penny had made me realise that I needed to have a little chat of my own with someone...

33

SARAH

As I climbed back up the path towards the village, I had a renewed sense of purpose. Talking to Penny had bolstered me. Our chat had helped me to cast a spotlight on my own problems. It wasn't just Penny who had needed to hear those words; they had given me cause for reflection too.

Greg and I had something wonderful together. In the eighteen months since he had come into my life, he had made me happier than I had ever believed possible, and I couldn't let our disagreement fester out of control. We were bigger than that. I owed it our marriage to sort this out now. I believed that if we sat down, talked properly and listened to one another, then we could reach a compromise. Greg was a good man. I was sure that if he understood how I was feeling, he might be able to see my point of view.

I pushed open the wooden gate. Gareth stood up from the windowsill and arched his back when he saw me. I reached out to rub his tabby fur. Then, taking a deep breath, I opened the door.

Greg was sitting at the kitchen table, hunched over his laptop and surrounded by a sea of paperwork.

'Greg,' I ventured.

He stopped typing and looked up at me. 'We need to talk —' he said, before I had a chance to say the same words that I had been rehearsing in my head the whole way home.

'We do,' I agreed.

He closed his laptop, pushed it away, then he pulled out a chair for me to join him at the table, and I crossed the kitchen and sat down opposite him. I could see in his eyes that he hated all of this and I guessed that he wanted to sort this out as much as I did. I couldn't help feeling a surge of love for him.

'Greg, I hate this,' I began. 'I hate us being on bad terms. It isn't *us*.'

He nodded sheepishly. 'I do too. It's been on my mind constantly; I've been messing up the orders all week in work. It's all I've been able to think about...'

'Having a family with you is all I could have ever dreamed of. One baby would have been perfect, but to be doubly blessed feels miraculous. We should be savouring every minute of this magical journey we're on together. I want you by my side throughout it all, and I don't want to look back sadly or to have it tarnished because we couldn't be adult enough to work through our problems.'

'I'm sorry, Sarah. I guess I just want everything to work out okay.'

'This isn't just your fault. I don't think either one of us is right or wrong ... I think we both want the same thing, which is to get this pair' – I placed my hands on my bump – 'here safely. I've been doing a lot of thinking and trying to understand your point of view, and I thought I would try to explain where I'm coming from.' I paused and took a deep breath. 'I love being pregnant, I really do, but I also feel a lot of pressure. It's like I've been tasked with minding the world's most valuable jewels, and I'm worried that if anything goes wrong that it'll be all my fault and I don't think you'd forgive me,' I blurted.

Greg's mouth fell open. 'Is that really what you think? But, Sarah, I could never think that. I know it's harder for you being the one who is pregnant but we're in this together, no matter what the outcome. It won't be your fault if things go wrong.'

'I know it sounds crazy, but that's how I feel.' I twiddled with a loose string on a placemat. 'A large part of me is still shocked to be pregnant, and I don't feel that I deserve all this good fortune. I hear a voice in my head telling me that something is going to go wrong and that I'm silly for believing that I could ever have all this.'

'But that's ridiculous, Sarah.' He looked aghast.

'I know. I never said it made sense, but that's how I feel. Honestly, I'm terrified. At least when I'm busy in work, my head is a little less scary because I don't have as much time to think about everything that could go wrong.'

'But why didn't you say something before?' His face was filled with concern. He reached across the table and placed his hand over mine. My skin tingled. I had missed his touch so much.

'Maybe because I've never seen you look so happy,' I said. 'Ever since I told you that I was pregnant, you've been going around with a big happy smile, assuming that everything will work out okay, and I love seeing you like that.'

'But you've shouldered all this worry on your own! You should have told me, and I could have tried to help. I feel like I've been so insensitive to all your worries.'

'I guess I just couldn't bear to take that excitement away from you.'

'But we have to stay positive that it'll all work out okay, or else what's the point?'

I shook my head. 'I wish I could, but unfortunately I'm a worrier by nature and, until these babies are here, I can't take anything for granted. Maybe it's because I lost Dad when I was young. I know how easily things can go wrong.'

'Oh, Sarah.' He got up from his chair, walked over and put his arms around me, pulling me in towards him. Under my cheek, his heart beat steadily. 'I've been a selfish jerk, I'm sorry. I wish you'd told me all of this sooner so I could have tried to be more understanding.'

I shook my head. 'I love your enthusiasm and ridiculous sense of optimism. It makes me hopeful, so please don't ever change. Somebody needs to balance up my Pessimistic Pamela.'

'I need to apologise for giving you a hard time about going to work. When I was growing up, Mom always said that life could turn on a dime, and I got a fright that day when we had to go to the hospital. I guess I was trying to do the impossible. I just wanted to have some control in a situation where we have no control. I know you'd never jeopardise the pregnancy if you thought there was any risk. I'm sorry. I never should have doubted you.'

'It's okay, I'm sorry too. I shouldn't have stormed out that morning. We should have discussed it properly like adults and it would never have blown up into this big tiff.'

'I love you, Sarah,' he said, kissing me on the lips. 'I've been so miserable over the last few days. No more fighting, deal?'

'Deal,' I agreed as he pulled me close. 'Now, let's enjoy these last few weeks before all the craziness really starts!'

We flopped down onto the sofa. Greg flicked on the TV and I snuggled into him. We caught the end of the weather forecast, which showed a storm tracking across the Atlantic, due to make landfall in the next few days. I tensed. Living in a coastal village on the westerly tip of Europe meant that storms hailing from the Atlantic were part and parcel of life, but I had always hated the unpredictable nature of storms. Sometimes they would lose power before they reached land, or would track off in a different direction altogether, but there were many times when the village had been damaged by floods and storm-force winds.

'I hate storms,' I said, cuddling closer to Greg.

'I think we've had enough storms here over the last few days, so let's hope this one passes over us.'

34

I heard Joe's footsteps coming down the hall towards the kitchen. As he got closer, I felt my stomach lurch, and feared that my breakfast might come back up again. *Stop being ridiculous, Penny, you're doing the right thing,* I reminded myself.

Sarah's words from the day before were still ringing in my ears. She had been right about living life with no regrets. I knew that if I didn't give my marriage another chance, I might regret it forever. How would I ever be able to look Lucy in the eye, knowing that I hadn't tried my best to work things out with her father?

So, despite the sick feeling in the pit of my stomach, over the last couple of days I had started to gather my belongings and fold my clothes into piles before packing them into my small case. It was time to go home.

'Good morning,' Joe said as he came into the kitchen. Mam was at the sink washing the dishes, while Dad dried them. Joe came over and greeted me with a kiss on the cheek before joining me at the table. 'How did you sleep, sweetheart?' he asked.

'Great,' I lied.

He was in his dressing robe. His curly dark chest hair peeped through above the V where the fabric crossed over. He reached out to take Lucy, but she stayed clinging to me. Disappointment registered in his eyes. She still hadn't entirely warmed to her father, much to his chagrin. He was trying hard, in fairness to him, and I could sense his growing frustration. I had told him to be patient with her, but it was going to take time to repair their bond. It would be easier when it was just the three of us again, I told myself.

'There's a fry for you in the grill,' Mam said as she scrubbed a pot.

'Thanks, Rita,' Joe said, standing up and taking the plate. 'So today's the day, then.' He sat back down at the table and beamed at me. 'I must say I'll miss these breakfasts.' He cut into a thick slice of bacon.

The day had finally arrived for our return to Dublin. I couldn't delay it any longer: the time had come for us to depart the village. Just like the last of the holidaymakers, who were locking their holiday homes until the following year, and the leaves, which were starting to dance down from the branches in colours of mustard and rust, signalling the end of another Inishbeg Cove summer, it was time for me to say goodbye to the village.

I smiled across the table at him. I knew Joe was excited by the idea of having us all back in our own house again, and for his sake I was doing my best to look happy. Try as I might, I couldn't find words for what I was feeling. Was it simply apprehension? Worry for the future of my marriage, maybe? Or perhaps it was because I would desperately miss my parents. I would miss the village too, of course, and Ruairí and the café. *And Tadgh*, a little voice whispered before I silenced it.

'I must say I'm looking forward to getting back home,' he continued. 'The village is lovely, but it gets claustrophobic after a while.' He laughed.

Mam snorted. 'I've the last few bits of Lucy's clothes on the line. They won't be long drying with that wind. I just hope that storm holds off for a while...'

'Thanks, Mam,' I said, suddenly feeling emotional. I knew washing Lucy's clothes before I packed them was a small gesture, but it represented how thoughtful my mother was. Even though I was thirty years of age, she still liked to mammy me, and I liked letting her do it. There was something about having her around that made me feel as if I was wrapped in a warm blanket, no matter how old I was. Mam had been so good to us over the summer. She had got me through some really difficult days. When I had been unable to function, Mam had stepped in and taken over the reins until I was feeling better.

'We're going to really miss you both, especially this little lady,' Dad said, walking over from the sink. He dried his hands on his tea towel before bending down and lifting Lucy up. If Joe noticed how readily she went into my father's arms, his face didn't show it.

With shock, I noticed tears glistening in Dad's eyes. Dad rarely cried. I had to look away, afraid I wouldn't be able to keep my emotions in check.

'I know we can't hang on to ye forever,' he continued, a tremor in his voice, 'but it has been the best summer having you both here. Having little Lucy in the house has brought so much joy to our lives. Thank you, Penny.'

'I know, Dad,' I said, tears shining in my own eyes. 'We've loved it too, but we'll have all the good memories we made to keep us going, hey?'

'We do, love,' he agreed.

'And there's always FaceTime,' Joe added.

'I don't think we'll be doing much of that,' Dad muttered.

I knew Joe meant well, but he didn't really understood how hard this was for Mam and Dad. And me.

'I no wanna go to our house,' Lucy protested.

'Of course you do, sweetheart,' Joe cajoled.

'No, I don't,' she said, shaking her head defiantly. 'Me like Ganny and Gandad's house.'

It felt as though all the air was being sucked from the room. I could hear Joe's voice in the background, trying to persuade Lucy that she would enjoy going home. Everything faded to a blur. I needed to get some air – just a few minutes alone. To tell myself that I was doing the right thing. I knew I was, so why did my heart feel so heavy?

I pushed back my chair. Everyone turned to look at me.

'Are you okay, Penny?' Mam asked, her face etched with concern.

I nodded. 'I just want to run up to the café to say goodbye to Ruairí before we go.' I stood up from the table. I felt suffocated and needed to escape.

'Well, don't be long. We need to get on the road before that storm arrives,' Joe warned.

'I won't.' I leant across and gave him a kiss on the cheek, then headed out the door.

The clouds rolled under the eel-coloured sky and the sea was as still as a sheet of glass. No birds were cartwheeling; the gulls were silent; up on the headland, the cows all lay down. This was the calm before the storm.

The blood pulsed in my ears as I hurried out of the house. I took great gulps of air, letting it fill my lungs until my heartbeat began to slow down again. *You're doing the right thing, Penny,* I reminded myself.

Several of the business owners were drawing their shutters and boarding up their shop fronts. Mrs O'Herlihy struggled to take down the nets bulging with beach balls and bucket and spade sets that hung outside of her shop.

'Good morning, Mrs O'Herlihy,' I said as I passed her.

'Morning, Penny,' she called after me.

'It's a wild one,' I remarked, looking towards the sky, which was the colour of steel. Heavy clouds hung, ominous and threatening, above the village.

'Please God the forecasters have got it wrong and it won't cause too much damage,' she said nervously.

I carried on down the main street and saw Sarah's husband Greg standing on the back of a truck, passing sandbags down to some of the village men, who had formed a chain and were passing them along from one person to the next then carrying them along the street to help protect businesses from flooding. Growing up in the village, I had witnessed my fair share of storms over the years. I felt a sense of unease as I watched the villagers go about their preparations. I could tell they really were expecting a big one.

When I reached the café, I saw that Ruairí had piled sandbags up on either side of his door. I pushed it open, feeling a flood of sadness that this would be the last time I would be here for a while. I knew I would come back to visit him whenever I came home to see my parents, but it was the end of this chapter – a chapter that, in a strange way, I had enjoyed so much.

'Hi there,' I said. A gust of wind propelled me through the door, a flurry of leaves following in my wake.

'Ah, hi, Penny,' Ruairí said.

I struggled against the force of the wind to shut the door behind me. 'What's going on here?' I asked. He was lifting all the chairs onto the tables. The floor-level shelves behind the counter where we usually stored bags of coffee beans and boxes of napkins were empty.

'I'm just making sure I have the place ready in case the village floods.'

'You must be so worried,' I said. I knew this was a stressful time for the villagers, but especially for the business owners, who I guessed were in for a sleepless night.

He shrugged. 'We can prepare as best we can, but we can't hold back nature.'

'Fingers crossed it won't hit too hard.' I took a deep breath. 'I just came to say goodbye. Today is the day.'

He put down the chair he had just picked up, straightened up and looked at me, his head tilted to one side. 'So, you didn't change your mind?'

I shook my head. 'I have to try to work things out with Joe.'

He nodded. 'I have to say I admire you, Penny.'

'Thanks,' I mumbled, embarrassed. If only he knew the way I was really feeling inside. Torn, shredded and uncertain about the future. He wouldn't think so well of me then. 'Look, Ruairí,' I began. 'I want to thank you for everything you've done for me... You'll never understand how much this place meant to me.' In the few months I had been in the village, I had made new friends and got a job. People liked me here; they wanted to be around me. I realised that, although I had been pushed out of my comfort zone, I had really needed it. In my short time in the village, the old me had slowly started to emerge, and I knew I wasn't going home the same person I was when I had arrived.

'Well, it wasn't all one-sided, you know, Penny. You dug me out of a hole too.'

'Y'know, when Mam came home that day and told me I was starting work here, I was furious. I thought I was the one doing *you* the favour when I turned up that first day, but when I look back, I think it was the other way around. Working here was more than just a job to me – it helped me through a really dark time in my life and...' I paused before adding, 'and you've become such a dear friend to me.'

'Oh, come here, you.' Ruairí held his arms open. I ran into them and squeezed him hard. I felt tears burning behind my eyes.

'I'm really going to miss you,' I sobbed, mortified that I

was not in control of my emotions. Every time I thought of all I was leaving behind me, I felt loss so strongly within me. I was bereft. I hadn't even felt like this when I had left the village to go to college.

When I pulled back, tears were shining in his eyes too. 'Look what you've done,' he scolded me through laughter as he wiped his eyes. 'You've been a breath of fresh air in this place. I enjoyed having you as my sidekick every day. We were a kick-ass duo.'

'We were,' I agreed, thinking about all the fun we had together over the summer.

'Don't be a stranger; keep in touch. I'm always at the end of the phone if you want to chat … and you know there'll always be a job here for you if you need it.'

'Thanks, Ruairí,' I said wiping my dripping nose with the back of my hand. 'I appreciate it.'

'Oh, by the way, did you see Tadgh?'

At the mention of his name, my heart filled with soreness. 'No, why?' I shook my head, trying my best to sound nonchalant.

'Well, he was just in here looking for you—'

'He was?' My heart stumbled, and I hated myself for it. In just a few hours I would be going home to work on my marriage. I shouldn't be having these feelings for another man.

'Yeah, I told him you had already finished up because you were heading back to Dublin. He seemed a bit…'

'What?' I asked, holding my breath while Ruairí deliberated on the right word.

'A bit … disappointed, maybe.' He raised his eyebrows at me. 'I thought you would have told him you were leaving, to be honest.'

I had thought about calling to say goodbye to Tadgh, but

in the end had decided against it. What use would it be? Everything had already been said between us. I was going back to Dublin with my husband and there was no use prolonging it with drawn-out goodbyes. No, I was better off just leaving then we could both get on with our lives and forget about one another.

'Erm, I didn't get a chance. I've been so busy packing up and everything...'

He nodded.

'I'd better get on,' I said. 'Joe wants to hit the road before this storm arrives.'

'Goodbye, Penny,' he said pulling me into another hug. 'I really do hope it all works out for you.'

'Me too,' I said biting down nervously on my lower lip.

36

I left Ruairí's café and noticed that the wind had really started to pick up. It whipped loose strands of hair around my face as I walked. The villagers were still handing out sandbags and were using them to build a defence wall along the main street. I kept walking and was about to turn in the direction of my parents' cottage when something made me stop. Ruairí's raised eyebrows when I had told him I hadn't said goodbye to Tadgh were sitting uneasily with me. Through his facial expressions, he had mirrored the same doubts I had felt for the last few days. Could I really leave without saying goodbye to Tadgh? *Yes, you can. Just keep walking*, a voice inside me said, but then another voice, a louder one, said, *Don't you owe it to him to say goodbye properly?* I knew it would be easier to get in the car and head for Dublin and try to forget all about Tadgh but, as Dad always used to say to me when I was growing up, 'the easier thing to do isn't always the right thing'. I decided to walk up to the restaurant. If he was there, then I could say a proper farewell. If not, then at least I had tried, and I could return to Dublin with a clear conscience.

I glanced at my watch. Joe would be starting to wonder where I was. The steel-grey sky now had shades of charcoal and inky black, and it looked like it was about to spill with rain at any moment. The storm was close to making landfall so, if I was to go, I would need to be quick. Before I could talk myself out of it, I crossed over towards the cove and headed in the direction of the cliff path. The fishing boats were all moored in the harbour, and I watched as they rocked in the water.

The waves lashed and licked the cliffs below me, sending up spray. The wind blustered around me and several times I had to grip the safety railing – the only thing protecting me from falling down the sheer cliff – to protect myself. The wind caused the hood on my light rain jacket to balloon out around my ears, and it was difficult to make headway, such was its strength. Every so often I was showered by frothy seawater, drenching me, despite my jacket. This was crazy, I told myself. Walking along the cliff path in weather like this was sheer lunacy.

I was relieved when the restaurant finally came into view. A yellow light shone out from the porthole-shaped window like a beacon. I reached the door and tried to open it, but it was locked. I gave a knock and waited. There was no reply, so I tried again. Suddenly I began to doubt myself. Tadgh would hardly be here on a day like this, would he? But there was a light on... I was about to turn away when I heard his gravelly voice. 'Penny?'

'Tadgh—'

He looked taken aback to see me standing there. 'What are you doing up here in this weather? I thought you had already gone.'

'We're going today.'

'I thought you had left without saying goodbye.'

Heat crept into my face. 'I wasn't sure whether I should come or not...' I admitted.

'I'm glad you came, even if you are crazy coming up here in this weather,' he said, grinning ruefully.

His smile made my heart smile. I was suddenly soaked by a particularly forceful jet of sea spray that frothed over the cliffs. I screamed as the icy water dripped down inside my jacket.

'You'd better come inside outta that weather.' He ushered me into the sanctuary of his restaurant. I lowered my hood as the gale outside muted to a distant drone. Water ran from my hair down my face. There was no one else in the restaurant, which was eerily silent, apart from the raging wind beyond the door.

'You're hardly working on a day like today?' I said, wiping away the droplets that ran down my forehead.

'I'm just catching up on a few bits while the place is quiet. I'll head home soon. What time are you leaving at?'

'Joe is keen to get on the road before the storm, so I can't stay long.'

'Are you looking forward to going home?' he asked.

'To be honest, I think it'll be strange leaving the village after being here all summer, but it's the right thing to do.'

'And are you and Joe working things out?'

I nodded. 'I know it will take time to get things back on track, but...' I paused, searching for the right words. 'We're trying.'

His face clouded over. 'The timing never seems to be right for us.'

'What do you mean?'

He tilted his face towards mine, and our eyes locked. His cool blue eyes with their wild amber flecks were so clear and honest, like the purest spring water.

'When you showed up here after all these years,' he began, 'I realised that there was still something between us, then when you told me that you felt it too, part of me thought that maybe we'd have the chance to be together again. I don't know – it was like a sign that we were meant to be. I know it sounds stupid. I guess I'm just disappointed that it didn't work out for us. Again.'

'I'm sorry, Tadgh, but I have to at least try – for Lucy's sake. I have to give my marriage another shot.'

'I get that,' he said, shaking his head, a haunted look in his eyes. I couldn't help feeling that history was repeating itself. 'But seeing you again has made me realise that, ever since we broke up, I've been waiting for you. As much as I wish I didn't, I've never stopped loving you, Penny.'

I was blindsided. It was as if all my senses had faded to a blur – my sight, my smell, my hearing all became mute as I processed what Tadgh was saying. He said he *loved* me – that he had always loved me.

'Maybe if life hadn't thrown so much at you as a teenager, we could have had something great together,' I said softly. I could feel all my resolve melting away. What might my life have been like if Tadgh and I had stayed together – if I had never met Joe? An image of us, settled in the cove, flashed into my mind, as if I was watching a movie of how my life might have gone. How I longed to stay, for him to take me in his arms, and to finally give our relationship the chance it deserved to grow and flourish, but how could I do that? I was married to Joe and we had a daughter together. I had to do right by my family.

'So, you've thought about it too?' he asked, his eyes wide and searching. 'You've imagined what our life would have been like if we had stayed together?'

'Of course I have,' I admitted, feeling as though I was

being pulled onto dangerous ground, ground I wasn't sure I wanted to be on. I had made my mind up, but I knew my resolve was fragile and I didn't want my feelings for Tadgh to cloud my head once again. 'But we don't get to see what life could have been like, had we stayed together. We get one chance and we have to make the decisions we think are right at the time. And right now, I have to try to save my marriage.'

He sighed. 'I would never stand in the way of you working things out with your husband. I don't know. Maybe I just have to accept that we're just not meant to be...'

We exchanged sad smiles as silence fell upon us. There was nothing more to be said.

'I'd better go before this storm arrives,' I said eventually.

'I wish you all the best, Penny.' He moved closer to me. For a glorious moment, I thought he was going to kiss me, but instead his face brushed past mine, so close that I could smell his salt-scented skin, then he turned and walked deeper into his restaurant, away from me and out of my life once more.

Dusk was starting to fall by the time we were ready to leave the village. The wind swirled leaves around my feet where I stood on the footpath outside the cottage with my parents as they waited to see Joe, Lucy and me off.

The approaching storm grumbled over our heads, the gathered clouds threatening to burst at any moment. I watched as the waves breached the seawall, each wave sending up higher spray than the one before it. Suddenly the skies opened and rain began to fall, softly at first but quickly building into heavy rain, soaking our clothes instantly.

'Come here, love, it's time to go,' I said, trying to prise Lucy away from my mother, to whom she clung like a limpet.

'Me no wanna go home!' she wailed. Her voice came out muffled, as her face was buried in Mam's neck.

'Come on, sweetie,' I coaxed, but she refused to look at me. I felt my eyes fill with tears too. Between the emotional toll of saying goodbye to Tadgh up in the restaurant and now having to say farewell to my parents, I was having a difficult time keeping my feelings in check. I knew I could come undone very easily and seeing Lucy getting upset was not helping matters. As a mother there was something about seeing your child distressed that caused pain deep within your soul and made you want to fix it instantly, but this time I couldn't – the time had come for us to return to Dublin.

'Whisht now, *a leanbh*,' Mam whispered, cuddling Lucy and barely managing to disguise her own upset. 'Sure you must be excited to see all your toys ... and the fairies were telling me that all your dollies have been missing you.'

'I no wanna go, Ganny,' Lucy sobbed. Her damp hair clung to her tearstained face and the rain had already started to soak through her cotton dress, causing it to stick to her skin in transparent patches.

'Come on, Lucy,' Joe said with a little less patience than the rest of us were affording her. 'We're all getting drenched here.'

'We'll see each other soon, love. Your mammy promised she'd bring you down to visit us in a few weeks.' It was Dad's turn to cajole her, but Lucy was inconsolable.

'Come on, that's enough now, Lucy,' Joe said, more sternly this time. Then, without warning, he reached out and took her out of Mam's arms. He turned to me. 'I'll strap her into the car while you say goodbye. Don't be long – we need to get on the road before this weather gets any worse.'

I nodded while rain ran down my head and face. My heart twisted at the sight of my daughter kicking and screaming as Joe struggled to get her into the car.

I turned away from the car and looked back at my

parents, who suddenly looked older. This goodbye was clearly breaking their hearts too, but I knew they were trying to put on a brave face for my sake.

'Thanks, Mam and Dad, for everything. You've been brilliant,' I said, swallowing a lump in my throat and feeling a surge of emotion for my parents. They had been so good to Lucy and me over the summer, and I would sorely miss having them around. 'Spending the summer with you was ... so special.' Having spent a large portion of my adult life believing that life in Inishbeg Cove was stifling, I now realised how wrong I had been. The village was part of me. It would never leave me. Tears welled in my eyes. Suddenly I couldn't keep it in any longer. Despite my best efforts, I began to sob.

Dad threw his arms around me. For a brief moment I closed my eyes and just let myself be in the safe place that was my father's embrace. His hug was just as comforting to me now as it had been when I was a child.

'I know we can't keep ye here forever, as much as we wish we could, *a ghrá*,' Dad said. 'I hope you and Joe can work it out, but you know you'll always have a place here if you need it.'

'Thanks, Dad,' I choked out.

'Now you'd better get going before you get soaked.' He swallowed hard.

I reached out and hugged Mam tightly until the two of us were a sobbing mess then I reluctantly let go and walked towards the car. I could still hear Lucy screaming from her car seat through the glass. I took a deep breath, trying to steady myself before Joe saw how upset I was. He would be expecting me to share his excitement at heading back to Dublin. How could I explain how I was feeling?

'Take it easy, love,' Mam warned as they followed me. 'Make sure you tell Joe to stick to the speed limit.'

'I will,' I promised.

I opened the car door and sat in the passenger seat, listening to Lucy bawling behind me.

'Keep her between the ditches,' Dad said, clapping his hand on the car roof. I felt an acute wave of tenderness for my father. Dad had been saying this to me whenever I left the village for as long as I could remember. I usually rolled my eyes at his predictability, but this time it was different. I would miss all of his sayings – especially his time-worn ones – and the reassurance of his routines so much.

As Joe pulled out onto the road, I watched Mam and Dad getting soaked by the rain, which was hitting them in horizontal slants. They waved tearfully at us from the foot-path. Raindrops ran down the window, meeting other drops to form rivers. My stomach lurched. Lucy's wailing reached fever pitch in the back seat. Just then the whole sky lit up, as though someone was shining a lamp towards the clouds, as jagged streaks of lightning split the sky open. Thunder rumbled, filling my ears with the loudest roar.

Suddenly I realised I couldn't go through with it. I couldn't leave the village. Somewhere over the summer months, I had changed. I wasn't the same woman who had arrived here with a suitcase and a broken heart; I had grown and discovered more about myself than I had ever thought possible. I belonged in the village now. This was where I'd been born. I belonged here just as much as the sea did, rolling in and out of the cove day after day. It was in my blood.

'Wait—' I said to Joe.

'What's wrong?' he asked, turning to look at me across the gearstick. 'Did you forget something?'

'Stop the car!'

'What is it?' Irritation flashed in his eyes.

The words that I had tried to keep suppressed over the last few days came tumbling out of my mouth. 'I'm sorry, Joe but I just can't do it.'

The wind swirled around the cottage as I walked over to the window and pulled back the curtains once more to check if I could see anything. Raindrops clouded the glass, and the sea lashed the rocks beyond the window. The village appeared to be under a dark cloak. Greg and I had been sitting on the sofa watching the news when the TV screen had gone black and we were plunged into darkness.

Greg had jumped up and reached for the candles we had left on the table in case of a power cut. He struck a match and began to light them, and it wasn't long before the room was lit by a soft amber glow.

Not for the first time that evening, I'd thought about Mrs Manning. She was quite unsteady on her feet these days, and I didn't know how she'd manage with no electricity. Earlier in the day I had tried to persuade her to stay with Greg and me until the storm had passed, but to no avail. She could be quite stubborn when she wanted to be and said that she had lived through more storms than I had eaten hot dinners. She had said she'd go to bed early and it would all be over by the time she woke.

I turned to Greg. His angular features were highlighted by the candlelight. 'I really hope Mrs Manning is okay...'

'Do you want me to call to check on her?' he offered.

'Oh Greg, it's a bit risky going out in that weather—'

'She's only up the street. I'll be up and back in a few minutes.'

I bit my lip. 'I don't know, Greg...'

'I'll be ten minutes max.'

'Well, okay,' I said, feeling uneasy even as I agreed to it, 'but please be careful.'

That had been two hours ago. Now I was pacing around our cottage alone, waiting for him to return. To make matters worse, my phone was dead so I couldn't call him. I was really starting to think that something had happened to him. He could be trying to call me, not realising that my phone was out of charge. Then the other, more rational, part of my brain said that perhaps he had decided to stay with Mrs Manning to keep the old lady company. But I had no way of knowing, and my mind was racing with all the possible worst-case scenarios.

The candlelight sent shadowy flickers around the room. I thought about heading out to Mrs Manning's myself to see if I could find him, but it was risky going out in the storm. My bump meant that my centre of gravity was way off these days. If I tripped in the darkness or got injured by flying debris, I'd never forgive myself. I decided to wait a while longer. If he hadn't appeared in half an hour, I would have no choice but to brave the elements and try to find him.

I had a dragging, heavy feeling in my bump. I was just making my way back towards the sofa when I felt a trickle of liquid between my legs. I stopped dead. Surely that wasn't what I thought it was? But I didn't think I had wet myself... I tried to check as best I could in the dim candlelight but, when I bent over, there was an unmistakable gush, and I knew my waters had gone. Fear snaked through me. I was only twenty-six weeks pregnant. It was far too early. What the hell was I supposed to do now? Panic filled me, rooting me to the spot. I couldn't think straight. I had no phone, no way of checking with the hospital to see what I should do. I needed Greg. He was always calm in a crisis and would know what to do.

I made my way over to the press under the stairs and rooted around for the torch. I located it but, when I tried to switch it on, it didn't work. It must have needed new batteries. God only knew where they were. Damn it, I thought, tossing it back into the press.

I pulled on my rain jacket, although it wouldn't fasten over my bump. I had been meaning to buy a new one for the forthcoming winter but hadn't got around to it. I opened the door and the wind rushed inside the cottage as I headed out into the storm to try and find Greg.

Rain poured from the skies and the gale sucked the breath from my lungs as I made my way down the street. Trees were bent double in the wind, and the rain came at me horizontally. Water was pouring over the seawall like a river. Oh God, this was worse than I thought. The whole village would be flooded at this rate. I was walking straight into the wind as I made my way downhill towards the main street. I moved as fast as I could, but the weight of my bump made me struggle. My jacket flapped in the wind, offering scant protection, and I was already soaked by the rain, which quickly found its way under my clothes until my skin was drenched.

I continued downhill until I reached the main street

where, without realising it, I stepped into water that went up to my knees. I cried out in shock. I could see that the whole street was shimmering, almost magically, under a foot of water. It seemed that the sandbags hadn't been able to keep the floodwaters at bay.

Mrs Manning's house was at the far end of the main street. In normal circumstances it would have been less than a five-minute walk but, trudging through knee-deep water, it took a lot longer. I reached my post office, and my heart twisted when I saw that rainwater had breached the wall of sandbags built across the door. It was probably seeping underneath the door and across the floor inside. Up ahead, I saw a group of men struggling to reinforce the wall of sandbags. Perhaps Greg was helping them, I thought. That was the kind of thing he would do. I felt a renewed optimism and tried to hurry to reach them.

'Sarah, what are you doing out in this weather?' A man stood with his hands on his hips, surveying me. When I got closer, I realised it was Maureen's husband, Jim. I looked around at the other men but didn't see Greg among them. My heart sank.

'Have you seen Greg?' I asked.

He shook his head. 'He was helping us out here earlier in the afternoon all right, but he went home hours ago. Is everything okay?'

Suddenly I felt a vice-like pain across my abdomen, and I was unable to talk.

'Sarah, are you okay?' Jim asked.

'I think the babies are coming,' I said, feeling terror grip me. 'I don't know where Greg is – it's too early.'

'Okay, let's get you up to the B&B and we'll call an ambulance,' Jim said calmly. I was grateful to allow someone else to take control, and followed him up the street towards Cove

View, where he and Maureen lived.

Cove View, like many of the homes at this end of the street, was set at the top of a flight of granite steps, so the water hadn't managed to breach it.

'Maureen is in bed. Hang on until I wake her. She'll be more use to you than I will,' he mumbled apologetically.

Minutes later Maureen descended the stairs wrapped in a ruby-coloured dressing gown.

'Sarah, my God, are you okay, girl?' she asked as her eyes adjusted to the light.

I shook my head in despair. 'I think my waters have broken and now I'm getting contractions.'

Jim explained to her what had happened and said that I couldn't find Greg.

'Sit down there a minute,' she said, showing me into her living room. 'Hang on until I put a few towels under you.'

Jim looked mortified.

Maureen turned to her husband. 'Jim, call the ambulance. Sarah needs to get to the hospital now. Tell them she's only six months pregnant with twins, and it's urgent.' She didn't need to spell it out to me: a twin birth was high risk at the best of times, but if the babies were born this early, they would definitely need special care. To give birth to them outside a hospital would be catastrophic.

Jim returned a few minutes later. 'They've dispatched one, but with the storm, it could take a while.'

'Oh God,' I wailed as I was hit by another vicious pain. They were coming closer together and getting more painful each time. They seemed to have ratcheted up a level since I had entered the B&B, and Maureen began to coach me through my breathing.

'Can you call ... Greg ... please?' I asked, trying to catch my breath between contractions. I needed my husband; I knew he would sort this out.

'I've already done that, love, but his phone seems to be off, I'm afraid.'

I realised then that Greg's phone was probably dead like mine. Why hadn't we thought to charge them? We had thought of everything else in preparation for the storm: we had bought new candles and matches and had stocked the cupboards with food, yet we'd forgotten to charge our mobile phones.

'Can you ring ... Mrs Manning ... he might ... be there.' I tried to get the words out between contractions.

'I'll do it right now.' Jim hurried out of the room again. He seemed to be relieved to have a job to do. Maureen squeezed my hand. 'Don't worry, love, we'll find him. He won't be too far away in this weather.'

Jim came back a few minutes later, a worried expression on his face. 'Mrs Manning said he called over to check on her but that he left to go home to you two hours ago, and she doesn't know where he is.'

39

SARAH

I cried out between the worry of what Jim was saying to me and the incredible pain I was experiencing, the like of which I had never felt before. Something must have happened to him. It was the only explanation why he had left Mrs Manning's house two hours ago but had never made it home.

I didn't have time to dwell on it because I was assailed by another contraction, that felt as though it would split my body in two. Maureen stopped pacing the floor and began to rub my back.

'I don't think I've got much time...' I wailed.

'Oh, where is that bloody ambulance?' she cried. She walked over to the window and pulled back the curtains to see if she could see it coming.

'It won't be able to get through the water, Maureen – it's over a foot high,' Jim said.

'Will you call them again? Look at her, Jim' – she pointed at me – 'she won't hold out much longer. They need to get here soon!'

Jim left the room again and returned a while later, more

grim-faced than the last time. 'The ambulance is stuck about five miles from the village. It can't get through the water. They're dispatching the helicopter to airlift her to the hospital, but we need to get her up onto high ground so it can land. I told them we'd meet them up on the headland.'

Maureen looked aghast. 'We can't expect Sarah to trek up there in this state, Jim!' she protested.

'We've no choice,' Jim said, shaking his head. 'We either get up to that headland or else...'

His unfinished sentence galvanised me into action, I had to do this for my babies. The alternative – well, it didn't bear thinking about.

'Come on, love,' Maureen soothed. 'Between us, we'll get you up there.'

I linked their arms and we stepped outside onto the main street. The water seemed to have risen in the short time I had been inside the B&B. I glanced around, hoping to catch sight of Greg, but he was nowhere to be seen. I was terrified that something awful had happened to him. Why else had he not arrived home after leaving Mrs Manning's? What if he had fallen and been submerged under the floodwater somehow or was trapped somewhere?

Maureen and Jim supported me as we began to wade through the water towards the dunes that led up to the cliff path. The wind howled and raged. At times we all had to stop to catch our breath as we didn't have the strength to fight through it. Sometimes I would have to drop Jim and Maureen's grip as I bent double with pain.

'You're nearly there now,' they encouraged me. I wondered if Maureen was thinking of her younger sister Della, Greg's birth mother, who had once made the same arduous trip up the headland while in the throes of labour.

The irony – that I was walking in the footsteps of the woman who had given birth to Greg – wasn't wasted on me.

'There's no sign of that chopper,' Jim said, anxiously scanning the sky. 'They said it had already been dispatched. It shouldn't take that long, surely?'

'Please God, it'll be along shortly,' Maureen reassured him. She gave my hand a squeeze. I knew she was trying to stay positive for my sake.

'I can feel pressure,' I cried out.

'Oh, sweet Jesus! Jim, ring them again and see where the hell it is!' Maureen's hair clung to her face and she looked wretched with worry.

Jim took out his phone and tried to talk to the operator once more, but it was difficult with the wind howling in his ears.

'I think they said it should be here in a few minutes, but I could hardly hear what they were saying,' he confessed.

I hung on to Maureen as my body was seized by pain. I seemed to be getting no break between contractions, and I didn't think I could hang on for much longer. What if my body just couldn't keep the babies in any more?

'Listen!' Jim cried.

I heard the welcome thrum of rotor blades coming towards us.

'There it is.' He pointed. In the distance a beam of light cut a path through the sky like a beacon. Relief flooded through me as the helicopter swooped in over the headland. Its giant blades were deafening even above the roar of the wind and its searchlight scoured the ground, presumably searching for us. Jim and Maureen began waving frantically in the hope they would see us, and it wasn't long before the helicopter was hovering above us. We watched it wobble in the wind as it attempted to descend, then it lurched to the right. The crew steadied it and tried again but again it tipped right in the wind. It tried once more, but it seemed that the crew couldn't hold it steady enough to land. I felt sick thinking what would happen if they couldn't land. *Please, Mam and Dad*, I found myself praying to my deceased parents. *Please let this helicopter get me and my babies to safety.*

I watched in dismay as the helicopter ascended again, leaving me stranded on the headland. My heart sank.

'Where the hell are they going?' Jim shouted angrily at the sky.

If they left me here, I knew there was no hope for my babies. This was it: my future hinged on this moment. All my hopes and dreams of having a family with Greg had been reduced to this single minute in time. We watched as the helicopter turned around and tried the descent again from a different angle. This time, miraculously, the helicopter stayed steady. Jim and Maureen screamed with delight when eventually it landed on the grass in front of us.

Once the blades had stopped rotating, Jim and Maureen helped me make my way towards the helicopter. Pain racked my body and the pressure between my legs was terrifying. The crew took over and helped me climb into the helicopter.

I said a hasty goodbye to Maureen and Jim, who promised me they would find Greg and tell him what had happened.

Then I was strapped in and hooked up to gas and air, which the paramedics said would take the edge off the pain. As the helicopter tried to take off again, we were all tossed from side to side inside. Eventually it found an even keel and as I inhaled the Entonox with each contraction, I felt as though I was floating over the bay.

As the helicopter headed for the hospital, I could hear a conversation taking place over the staticky radio.

'Rescue 116, do you receive me?' a voice said.

'Roger.'

'Whereabouts are you, Rescue 116?'

'En route to Limerick Hospital, ETA 23.10. Over.'

'We have another casualty in Inishbeg Cove. A male has been found unconscious under a fallen tree. Over.'

My heart stopped beating as the operator continued to talk.

It was Greg.

40

I t felt as though I was on fire: as if I had been lit from the inside and the flames were spreading throughout my body. The contractions wrapped themselves from the front of my abdomen, around to my back and back out the front again, moving down my body in endless waves.

'Just one more push, Sarah, and you'll be holding your baby. I can see a thick head of dark hair. You're so close now, lovey, come on, you can do it!' Ciara, my midwife, coached me. They had called Dr McCabe, my obstetrician, and she was on her way apparently. Ciara had been by my side since I had been lifted out of the helicopter and rushed down to the delivery suite, where a team of midwives and paediatricians waited. When she had learnt about Greg, she had quickly shifted from the role of midwife into the role of birthing partner too. She was encouraging me, holding my hand and calming me down when it all felt like too much.

I put my trust in her and did as she instructed. I gritted my teeth and pushed down with all my might, until finally I felt something warm slip out between my legs.

'It's a little girl!' Ciara called out. My heart seemed to

expand inside my chest as I caught sight of a tiny pink baby
with a shock of dark hair. She was whisked over to one side
of the room, where a team in green scrubs were waiting to
take care of her. She was so small. I gasped when I saw that
she fit into the cupped hands of the paediatrician who had
taken her from Ciara. Seconds seemed to last an eternity as I
waited to hear her cry but there was just silence.

'Is she okay?' I asked Ciara.

'Sometimes babies born this early can't cry yet so don't
be alarmed. The team are giving her the best of care. Now,
lovey, I'm sorry to have to do this to you again,' Ciara apolo-
gised, 'but we need to get this other baby out. We don't want
to leave it too long. So I need you to start pushing again,
Sarah.'

I was brought back to the reality of the situation. I had to
give birth for the second time. My body was shattered after
delivering the first twin, and the thought of summoning up
all that effort and energy once more was overwhelming.

'I don't think I can do it.' I shook my head and pushed
back the damp hair that was matted to the sides of my face.

'Yes you can, Sarah. I know you're exhausted, but you're
nearly there now. Your daughter is missing her buddy.'

My daughter. The sweetest words imaginable. The words
I had longed to hear for so long.

'It'll be the best thing you can do for her,' Ciara continued. 'They're twins – they don't like being separated.'

I had to find the energy to do this – I had to do it for my
babies. For Greg. My need to help my daughters cut deep
into my soul. I summoned every ounce of strength I didn't
think I had left and pushed down until I felt a hard round-
ness between my legs for the second time. I pushed again, the
strongest one of all, and felt my second baby slip out of me.

'Another little girl, Sarah,' Ciara cried out. 'Well done, superwoman!'

This time I heard a very weak, primal wail that told me she was here, she was alive, and she needed me. I knew then that she was going to be the bolshy one of the pair. Relief flooded through me. I watched, awestruck, as my second dark-haired beauty was placed alongside her sister. Just as Ciara had promised, both babies began to settle as soon as they were reunited. As the paediatricians took care of them, I was shocked by how tiny they were. Since they were premature, I had expected them to be small, but they were impossibly tiny.

'Their daddy will be blessed amongst women,' another of the midwives announced to the room. Ciara glanced nervously at me.

My euphoria was short-lived, as I was suddenly reminded of Greg. In the rush of being airlifted to the hospital, whisked straight to the delivery suite and giving birth to two babies with minutes of arriving, I had been temporarily distracted, but now, as I thought of him lying somewhere unconscious, possibly dead, my happiness evaporated and was replaced with despair. Horrible images flooded my mind. Had he been found? If so, had he been transferred to hospital yet? Or, what if— No, I couldn't let my head go there just now.

'Has there been any word yet?' I asked Ciara. She had told me she would update me as soon as the helicopter carrying Greg, arrived at the hospital. I had made her promise either way that she would tell me the truth: whether it was good news or not, I needed to know how he was.

Ciara shook her head. 'Not yet, but I've flagged it with

the A&E team. As soon as that helicopter lands, they'll let me know. They know how urgent it is.'

I flopped back against the pillows, tears burning in my eyes.

'It might not be as bad as you think, lovey,' Ciara assured me, 'so try to stay positive.'

I could tell she was anxious too and was just saying it to make me feel better.

'Now we need you to say goodbye to these little ladies for a while. The paeds are going to take them up to the Neonatal Intensive Care Unit.'

'Will they be okay?' I asked.

'They're in the best hands, Sarah. You have to remember they are very premature, and they need help with their breathing. Unfortunately there are no guarantees with babies born at this gestation, but the team will do everything that they can for them.'

A tear wound its way down my face as they wheeled my babies out of the room. I didn't think I had ever felt so alone. This wasn't how it was supposed to be. Somehow one of the best moments of my life had become one of the worst. I sank down in the bed, exhausted. My heart was sore for Greg. He should have been there. I needed him right now. He would have been overjoyed to see his daughters being born.

I knew bad news was coming. I could feel it looming ahead of me, like an oncoming train. I was sure I'd caught a glimpse of it on Ciara's face earlier – I think she already knew Greg's fate, but she didn't want to tell me just yet.

Rain lashed against the kitchen window. It sounded as though someone was flinging pebbles at the glass. Several times, I thought it might actually shatter from the force. From the living room, I could hear the wind howling down the chimney. The power had gone out several hours before, and we were sitting in candlelight around the kitchen table.

Lucy was conked out on my knee, her mouth half-open. Despite the blanket that Dad had thrown over the pair of us, I sat shivering on the kitchen chair as I tried to come to terms with the evening's events.

Saying goodbye to Joe and telling him the truth about how I felt and that I believed our marriage was over had been awful. His face had changed from shock almost straight to anger as he registered what I was telling him. In the end he had blazed that 'the shithole of a village was welcome to me' before storming out of the house. I had followed him, begging him to at least wait until the storm had passed before leaving. Despite everything that had happened, I still cared about him and didn't want him risking his life driving in a raging storm, but he climbed into the car, deaf to my pleas, slammed the door behind him and drove away.

I still couldn't believe I had done it. But as soon as I had uttered the words, relief had flooded through me and I knew I had made the right decision. It felt as though a weight had been lifted off me and I could finally breathe again. I had no idea what the future held, but I had to trust that things would all work out for the best. I hoped that in time, when Joe had calmed down, perhaps we could have an amicable relationship for Lucy's sake.

I thought about Tadgh too, and how he might react when I told him that I was going to be staying in the village. I knew we would need to take it slowly, but I hoped that the timing was finally right for us to be together.

I let out a large yawn. As the shock started to subside, it was replaced with bone-numbing tiredness. I was exhausted.

'Why don't you get some sleep, love?' Mam suggested, placing her hand over mine on the kitchen table. 'Things won't seem as bad in the morning.'

There were still so many things to be worked out, and my head was spinning with all the decisions I'd have to make now that I was going to stay in the village, but they could wait until the morning. Tomorrow was the start of my new life.

42

My name was being called, somewhere on the periphery of my dream. I tried to resist the voice: such was my exhaustion. I just wanted to be left to sleep.

'Sarah,' the voice called again, more insistently this time.

My eyes flickered open, and I saw Greg's concerned face in front of me. I rubbed my eyes, wondering if I was hallucinating. Ciara had given me strong painkillers – perhaps they were having a bad effect on me.

'I'm so sorry,' he began. 'I got here as fast as I could.' He was breathless and sweat glistened on his brow.

'Greg?' I tried to sit up in bed, but pain shot through me. 'You're alive?'

'Of course I am. I'm so sorry for causing you to worry—'

'But you were unconscious – the helicopter – how are you here?'

'What are you talking about?' He looked puzzled.

'When I was being flown to the hospital, I heard them on the radio talking about another casualty – a man who had been hit by a falling tree in Inishbeg Cove. I thought it was you.'

'I think there's been a mix-up,' Greg said, shaking his head.

'But where were you, then?'

He instantly looked sheepish. 'Well, I went to check on Mrs Manning like planned, and I was on my way back to you when I met Ruairí on his way to help some of the villagers at the parish hall. Part of the roof had blown off and they were trying to put on a tarpaulin to stop the rest of it being ripped off by another gust. I was giving them a hand. I thought we'd be done in half an hour, but the wind made it impossible to secure. If I had known you'd go into labour, I never would have gone.' He hung his head. 'When Maureen and Jim found me, I tried to get here as soon as I could. They told me the helicopter had only left twenty minutes before so I thought, if I was quick, I might make it before you gave birth, but I underestimated the storm.' He shook his head. 'All the approach roads to the village were flooded, so I couldn't drive. Ruairí managed to find me a boat, and I had to row out of the village until I came to higher ground. Then I had to walk along the roads trying to hitch a lift but, as you can imagine, there wasn't much traffic out on a night like this. Eventually I saw a Garda car, and when I told them what had happened, they blue-lighted me all the way to Limerick. I'm sorry, Sarah. I've let you down. The biggest moment of both our lives, and I wasn't there for you.'

'I'm just so happy you're alive. I thought I was going to be raising our daughters on my own.' I sobbed from sheer relief.

'We had two girls?' His face lit up.

I had forgotten that all this would be news for him. 'We

did ... oh, Greg, you should see them! They were so tiny but perfect. They've masses of dark hair, like you.'

'Are they okay?'

I shook my head. 'Nobody will tell me. They're very premature, of course. They said they'd let me know as soon as they were stable, but I haven't heard anything since they went to NICU.'

'Well, let's hope they take after their amazing mom.' He reached out and kissed me. 'How are you feeling?'

He had used the word 'mom', and I suddenly realised that I was now a mother. 'I feel like I've been hit by a train, to be honest, but I'm so glad you're here. I had all kinds of terrible thoughts running through my mind. I thought you were dead, and the midwives were afraid to tell me!'

'Oh, Sarah, what you must have gone through all on your own...' He shook his head and I guessed he was having a hard time reconciling the events that had taken place that evening.

'You were doing a good thing and, look, our babies are here now. Let's just hope they'll get through it. They're so early, Greg,' I said worriedly.

The midwife, Ciara, entered the room pushing a wheelchair and did a double take when her eyes landed on Greg.

'Ciara,' I said by way of introduction. 'This is Greg, my husband.'

'You're looking remarkably healthy for a man who was knocked unconscious by a falling tree, requiring airlifting to hospital just a few hours ago,' she said, a wry smile playing on the corners of her mouth.

'It was a case of mistaken identity.' Greg laughed and we filled her in on the story. I felt guilt shiver through me. I had been too busy celebrating the fact that it wasn't Greg who had been injured to give much thought to the person who had actually been involved. It was somebody else from the village – and, in a place the size of Inishbeg Cove, we would certainly know them. Some other poor family would be getting the phone call that no one wanted to receive.

'I have some good news for you both. I've just had a phone call from NICU. Your babies are settled and are currently stable. I can bring you up to meet them, if you want?'

Greg's immediately jumped off the bed.

'I thought you might react like that.' She laughed.

I moved more gingerly, swinging my legs over the side of the bed, easing myself into the wheelchair but I was no less desperate to see our babies.

43

I woke the next morning to the sound of birdsong and the sight of sunlight. I got out of bed, walked over to the window and pulled the curtains back to see a brilliant blue sky. The sea was as still as glass and tranquillity had been restored to the village once more. The previous day's maelstrom could almost have been a figment of my imagination. Mam was right: things didn't seem quite so bleak as they had the night before. I had been worried I would wake up feeling full of regret for being so impetuous, but I actually felt a bubbling sensation, a mixture of exhilaration and excitement, that I was embarking on a new phase in my life.

Lucy was still sleeping peacefully. I sat down on the edge of the bed and stroked her perfect skin, which was as smooth as velvet. This was not just the dawn of a new day, but the dawn of a new era in both our lives. I just hoped I was doing the right thing for her – but every cell within me told me we belonged in the village.

I left Lucy to sleep and went down to the kitchen. Out of habit I flicked the switch on the kettle but, when it didn't fire up, I realised that the electricity was still out. While the rest of the house was still asleep, catching up from our late night, I decided to take a walk up the main street to see how the village had fared during the storm.

I stepped outside to see that the sky was washed clean, but rivers of water ran down either side of the street as the floodwater receded back towards the sea. I continued along the main street where gritty debris and bits of driftwood tangled in seaweed, lay strewn around the road. I saw several business owners standing outside their shops wearing gloomy expressions as they counted the cost of the storm. I knew many of them couldn't get insurance cover because of the village's history of flooding. These businesses were their livelihood and, in a place the size of Inishbeg Cove, most of them barely turned a profit. Many of the businesses here weren't commercially viable and instead were run on a break-even basis for the benefit of the villagers. Further along I saw Mrs O'Herlihy crying and shaking her head as she surveyed the damage in her shop. I looked at the devastation all around me, heartbroken to see the village in this state. It would take months for the businesses to recover, if they ever did. I suddenly thought about Ruairí, and decided to walk on towards the café to see how he was doing. I desperately hoped he had managed to avoid being flooded.

I found him standing just inside the café door, using a yard brush to sweep murky brown water out of the café onto the footpath outside.

'Ruairí, I'm so sorry,' I said as I looked around at the devastation. The wood running along the bottom of the counter was starting to come away and warp as the water soaked into it. It would cost thousands to repair the damage.

'I thought you had left,' he said, stopping for a moment and resting on the handle of his brush.

'It's a long story.' I shook my head. 'The village really took a hammering.'

'Well, I'm counting my blessings this morning. I think I got away pretty lightly, all things considered.'

'What do you mean?' I was confused by his positivity. His business was in tatters – how was he able to look on the bright side so soon? Surely he was entitled to be angry and concerned for the future? I was devastated seeing the café in this state, and it wasn't even my business. He was a better person than I was, I thought.

His brows furrowed in surprise. 'Didn't you hear the news?'

'What news?'

'About Tadgh?' he continued.

The blood seemed to still in my veins. My senses seemed to sharpen: every sound was heightened. I could hear my heart hammering inside my rib cage.

'No, what happened?' My breath caught in my chest. I really hoped he wasn't going to give me bad news.

'He was hit by a falling tree on his way back from the restaurant last night. Senan found him, but they reckon he'd been lying there for a few hours at that stage. Then the ambulance couldn't get into the village because the road was flooded. Eventually they got him airlifted to Limerick Hospital. He's in intensive care.'

'Oh my God.' I gasped, feeling as though Ruairí had just punched me in the gut. I struggled to catch air and my legs grew weak. 'I need to get to him,' I said, turning and hurrying out of the café.

～

'WHAT'S WRONG, love? You look shook!' Mam said as I breathlessly rounded the kitchen door a few minutes later.

'Tadgh ... hospital ... I need to get to him.' The words felt staccato and disjointed as they left my mouth. I began to fumble around the kitchen, searching for my car keys.

'What on earth are you saying?' Mam asked, confused by my behaviour.

'Tadgh is in hospital,' I repeated.

'My goodness, what happened to him?' Mam asked.

'Apparently he got hit by a falling tree. He's in intensive care.'

'Oh Lord, save us!' Automatically, she reached up to her forehead and made the sign of the cross. 'Joe took your car, remember?' She lifted Dad's car keys off the hook hanging at the end of the run of cupboards. 'Here, take your father's car,' she said, handing me the keys. 'I'll mind Lucy but be careful, Penny – there will be a lot of trees down and flooding on the roads still.'

'I will. Oh, and Mam, I love you,' I added as I hurried out to the car.

44

The drive to Limerick Hospital was interminable. Dad's small car seemed to choke and stall up every hill and I came upon several fallen trees, requiring me to swerve to avoid them. My mind kept going to Tadgh and I had to wipe away tears so I could see the road before me.

Every time I thought of him lying there, alone in the raging wind, injured and with rain pelting down on him, tears streamed down my face. I imagined him crying out for help, his calls going unanswered until he was too weak to do so any more. Horrible images of his crushed, broken body filled my head. Intensive care meant his injuries were serious. I had tried phoning his younger brother Senan but there was no answer from his phone, and when I called the hospital nobody was able to give me an update on Tadgh's condition.

Between my worry for him and the treacherous driving conditions, my heart felt as though it was in my mouth by the time I finally pulled into the car park of Limerick Hospital.

I parked the car at a jaunty angle compared to the ones around it, but I didn't have time to worry about it. I hurried into the hospital building.

At the reception desk, I explained who I was but was told that, because I wasn't a family member, they couldn't give me an update on his condition. Instead I was directed to the intensive care waiting area.

I hurried along the rubber floor, where porters wheeled trolleys and nurses and doctors hurried past. When I reached the waiting room, I went inside. It was empty apart from a young, broad-chested man who was anxiously pacing the floor. He had the same jutting jawline and dark colouring as Tadgh, and I guessed it was his younger brother Senan. When I had last seen him, many years ago, he was a wiry child with sandy-coloured hair, but now he had grown into a well-built young man.

'Senan?' I asked.

He stopped pacing and looked at me.

'I'm Penny Murphy. I don't know if you remember me?'

'Of course I do. Tadgh told me you were back in the village...'

'How is he?' I asked.

He shook his head. 'No one will tell me.' He began to pace once more. 'He's all I have left. If anything happens him...' He broke off and his shoulders began to heave as tears took over. Senan and Tadgh had a bond stronger than that of most brothers. Tadgh had raised Senan from the age of six after their parents had died, and they were almost like father and son in many ways.

I walked over to him. Even though we barely knew one another, I couldn't help putting my arms around him. 'I'm sure he'll be fine. You know what Tadgh is like – he's the strongest man I know.'

'You didn't see him though, Penny... That tree – God, the size of it! It was so heavy; I couldn't get it off him. He was just lying there, all b-b-broken and twisted...' His face creased in pain. 'I should have gone looking for him sooner. I just thought he was still in work, y'know? But then when the storm got really hairy, I began to worry. I know Tadgh is a workaholic and he thinks he's invincible, but I knew even he wouldn't stay out in that weather, so I decided to head out and see if I could track him down. That's when I found him, lying near the bottom of the cliff path.' He broke down in tears as he relived the memory.

'That must have been awful for you, Senan.'

Suddenly a doctor in a white coat entered the room. Senan and I moved apart, each of us silently begging the man to give us the good news we so desperately wanted.

'Are you the family of Tadgh O'Reilly?' he asked.

I studied his face for an indication of the news he was about to deliver, but it remained impassive. I guessed he was used to keeping his composure when dealing with patients' relatives.

Senan nodded. 'I'm his brother and this is...'

'Penny,' I said, helping him out. 'I'm ... er ... a friend.'

'I'm Dr McGowan. Sorry it has taken me so long to get to you but, as you know, Tadgh sustained quite an injury. He's just out of surgery and is currently stable. There is some swelling on his brain, so we've had to put him in an induced coma—'

'Oh God,' I whispered. This was worse than I thought.

'We hope that this will give his brain time to rest, reducing the swelling and lessening the risk of any long-term effects. He also has two broken ribs, a punctured lung, a broken arm and a fracture on his skull,' Dr McGowan said.

'Just tell me, will he be okay, Doctor?' Senan begged.

'Unfortunately, I can't answer that. We will start reducing the sedation shortly, in the hope that he will begin to wake up, but we won't know the real extent of his injuries until then. For now, you must be prepared for every outcome. With an injury like the one Tadgh has sustained, there may be brain damage or even spinal cord damage from the weight of the tree trunk that fell on him, which could result in paralysis. We've carried out scans which will give us a clearer picture and I will let you know once we have the results of those. I'm sorry I can't give you any positive news right now, but it's a waiting game until he wakes up and we know what we're dealing with.'

I felt as if the air had been sucked out of me. There were so many things to consider that hadn't even crossed my mind as I had driven to the hospital. I had spent so much time praying that Tadgh would still be alive, but I hadn't thought about all the other things that could go wrong. Would he wake up as the Tadgh we knew and loved, or would he be changed forever by the accident?

'You can see him now, if you would like,' Dr McGowan went on.

Senan nodded and began to follow him.

'You can come too,' the doctor said, turning to me.

We followed Dr McGowan down a series of corridors until eventually we arrived at a dimly lit room. Tadgh lay covered up to his abdomen with a starched white sheet. His head was shaved on one side and blue-black bruising covered his chest. A bandage circled his head, and a cast covered his forearm. Everything in the room was perfectly still apart from the intermittent beeping of equipment that surrounded his bed. The realisation of where I was, and why I was here, hit me like a train.

'You can sit with him a while,' Dr McGowan said before excusing himself.

Senan and I took seats beside his bed. Tadgh was so tough: he surfed in the Atlantic in all weathers, he ran up and down the hills surrounding the village, barely breaking a sweat, so it was difficult to see him looking broken and vulnerable, wires trailing from his body as he lay in the hospital bed. I was afraid to touch him in case I set off an alarm or did something to endanger him.

'You can hold his hand if you like,' the nurse attending him encouraged us, as if reading my mind.

I looked at Senan. He nodded that it was okay. I reached out for Tadgh's broad hand. Dark hairs peppered his tanned skin. My movements were delicate at first but when I felt the warmth of his skin against mine, I was reassured and encased his hand fully inside my own.

Come on, Tadgh, I begged him. *I'm here. You have to wake up.*

45

PENNY

S enan's eyelids grew heavy and drooped closed before he startled awake again. He was trying his best to stay awake, but he clearly needed rest.

'Why don't you go and lie down on the chairs in the waiting room and get some sleep? You've been awake for over thirty-six hours. I promise I'll call you if there's any change, no matter how small.' I had suggested this to him several times already, but he had refused every time.

He blinked once more. 'Okay, maybe I will. But please, if there is any change, come and get me no matter what. Promise?'

'Of course I will,' I agreed.

They had stopped the sedation several hours ago, and now it was just a waiting game. I knew the medical team was keen to see signs of Tadgh waking up. Dr McGowan had said the preliminary scan results from his brain and spinal cord looked good, but we couldn't get our hopes up until he woke. He told us that the faster he came around, the better his prognosis would be. They had explained to us that it was important to keep talking to him, even when it might feel pointless – often patients in a coma could hear their loved ones' voices, so Senan and I took it in turns to fill the silence in the room with silly stories and anecdotes that, under ordinary circumstances, we knew Tadgh would find funny.

The time we had spent at Tadgh's bedside had allowed me to think. How ironic life was: I had finally realised what I wanted but, now that I had found it, I was so close to losing it again. I loved Tadgh. I knew that, I had always known it, but I had spent so long trying to suppress those feelings. Now that I was alone with him, I finally had a chance to say what I had wanted to for so long.

'I feel like I have so much to tell you,' I began. 'I'm sure you guessed because I'm still here. I stayed in the village ... I couldn't leave in the end. I told Joe that our marriage is over. And, by the way, you were right about the timing never being right for us, because here I am, ready and waiting for you, and you're in a coma... It feels like the odds are always stacked against us. But Tadgh, I want you to know that I love you. I always have. They say you never forget your first love, but it's more than that with us... No one compares to you. I'm sorry it took me so long to get it together, but I promise you, if you just wake up – and of course if you'll still have me – I'm all yours. I think the timing could finally be right for us... Come on, Tadgh.' I squeezed his hand, using as much pressure as I dared. 'I need you to wake up.'

Tears rolled down my face and landed on the white sheets as I talked. 'Come on, Tadgh,' I begged. 'Let's do this, let's finally give *us* a chance.'

Nurses came in periodically to check on him. Each time they would lift his lids and shine a torch into his eyes to see if his pupils responded, or sometimes they would gently call his name to see if he could hear them, but then they would shake their head at me, looking disappointed, before leaving the room once more.

Senan came back into the room a while later. I knew by the short length of time he had been gone that he hadn't slept properly.

'Any change?' he asked, hope filling his red-rimmed eyes.

'No, but the nurse said it's still early days. He just needs more time.'

He nodded and took the chair beside mine at Tadgh's bedside.

'Did you sleep?' I asked.

He shook his head. His dark, wavy hair, so like Tadgh's, stuck up chaotically and dark circles hung beneath his eyes.

'You know, he was my idol when I was growing up,' he said. 'I was too young to have proper memories of our parents before they died, but I can't remember ever feeling as though I was missing out and that was because of Tadgh – in fact, I thought it was kinda cool having my older brother bring me to school and pick me up. My friends used to be so jealous of me.' He laughed before growing serious once more and turning towards me. 'What if he doesn't come through this, Penny? What will I do without him? He's not just a brother; he's like my mother and father. He's my whole family – he's everything to me.' He shook his head. 'I never told him that. I wish I had...' He broke down into heaving sobs, and I reached across and put my arm around his shoulders.

'You mean the world to him too, Senan. He's always telling me how proud he is of you. Tadgh will get through this; I know he will. I've never met anyone with as much determination and grit as he has. Life threw some fairly shitty things on his doorstep and somehow, he's always managed to pick himself up again. You might not know this, but back when we were teenagers, we had planned to go to college together in Dublin, but then everything changed after your parents' accident. Tadgh decided to stay in the village to look after you and take on the restaurant, but do you know something? He never once complained. He just took what life threw at him and got on with it. How many other teenagers would be able for that? He's a rock, and that's why I know he's going to get through this. I *know* he will,' I said, feeling my determination grow with every word that left my lips.

'God, I hope you're right, Penny,' Senan said, shaking his head.

I felt a presence in the room. When I looked up, a nurse was standing at the end of the bed.

'I'm sorry, but I need you both to go now and let Tadgh get some rest.'

'Of course.' We stood up and kissed Tadgh gently on the forehead before leaving him alone, lost in the depths of his coma.

Monitors, bleeps and wires was my first impression of the Neonatal Intensive Care Unit. So many things pulled at my attention, and I didn't know where to look.

A nurse walked over and shook our hands. 'You must be Sarah and Greg. I'm Martha, a neonatal nurse here. Your girlies are doing great,' she assured us. 'I know it seems overwhelming right now and it's still early days, but we take it one day at a time here and so far, so good.' She smiled at us. 'Come on, they're over this way.'

Greg and I followed Martha to an incubator where two tiny babies wearing nappies that swamped their small bodies, topped with tiny knitted hats that looked as though they belonged on dolls, were cuddling up to one another. Tubes and wires that Martha explained were helping them to breathe, trailed from their miniature bodies. *Our daughters.* These babies were ours. I burst into tears. The enormity of everything that happened over the last twelve hours – actually, over the last eighteen months – hit me. What a whirlwind life had been for us.

Greg put his arms around me, and tears glistened in his eyes as we stared in wonder through the glass at the babies we had created.

Greg turned to me. 'They're beautiful, aren't they?'

'So beautiful,' I agreed, barely able to get the words out. 'I still can't believe they're ours – that I'm their mother.'

'And I'm a dad,' Greg said in amazement.

One of the babies moved her fingers and we watched, mesmerised, as she curled it around her sister's hand.

'They're already best friends.' I smiled.

Greg turned to me and took me in his arms. 'I never thought I would get this lucky. Since the day we met, you've made me happier than I ever thought possible, but today – well, today has topped it all. A year and a half ago, my life was falling apart and now, I can't believe I have a wife and two beautiful daughters.'

'You've made a lot of dreams come true for me too, you know,' I said, leaning my head against his chest.

'I know we're only at the start of our journey, but I wanted to say thank you, Sarah - for everything - to have a family of my own is all I ever wanted.'

I was standing in the hospital coffee shop, my phone pinched between my ear and shoulder, while I poured milk into the two takeaway Americanos that I had bought for Senan and me. I was talking to Mam. I had been feeling guilty for running out on Lucy when I had got the news about Tadgh's accident, and I was worried that after everything that had happened, she might be upset or confused, but Mam reassured me that she was doing great and was delighted to still be in the village. I had tried calling Joe to see if he had got home all right, but he hadn't answered my calls. Despite everything that had happened between us, I hoped he was okay.

While I was getting the coffees, Senan was sitting with Tadgh. At least one of us was always with him whenever the nurses allowed him to have visitors.

I was walking down the corridor clutching the coffees, heading back to Senan, when I spotted a familiar figure. I was sure it was Sarah O'Shea's husband Greg, but what was he doing at the hospital?

'Greg?' I called out. Although I didn't know him well, I felt I should check to make sure everything was okay.

He looked as if he was in a daze but came to at the mention of his name and turned to look at me. He looked surprised to see me standing there.

'Penny, isn't it?' he said. He looked rather dishevelled: his usually neat hair was unkempt, and his clothes were creased and wrinkled.

I nodded. 'What are you doing here?' I asked, then felt guilty for being so nosy. It wasn't any of my business.

'I was just going to ask you the same thing,' Greg replied with a friendly grin and I knew he hadn't taken offence.

'You may not have heard, but Tadgh was hit by a tree during the storm – he's in intensive care.'

'Oh my God, I'm sorry. Now it all makes sense – Sarah went into premature labour with the twins during the storm, and when she was being airlifted to hospital, she heard that someone in the village had been injured by a falling tree, but we didn't know who it was,' Greg explained. 'Will he be okay?'

'It's a waiting game, unfortunately. How is Sarah? And the babies?'

'She's recovering, and the babies are doing okay. They're three months early so they're in the NICU. We've been told to take one day at time, but fingers crossed – so far, so good. I think we're both in shock that they're here so soon, to be honest.'

'You must have got an awful fright. Please pass on my regards to Sarah, won't you?'

He nodded. 'And I'm thinking of you guys. I'll be praying for Tadgh.'

'Thanks, Greg. I'd better get back.'

I continued on towards Tadgh's room.

'Any change?' I asked Senan, handing him the coffee when I got back to Tadgh's bedside.

Senan shook his head. Asking if there had been any change in Tadgh's condition as soon as we returned was a habit Senan and I had fallen into but now, as time ticked on and Tadgh was showing no signs of coming to, I was starting to worry. I had deliberately pushed all the worst-case scenarios Dr McGowan had warned us about out of my head up to now. I knew Tadgh had a long journey ahead of him and I was prepared to be there with him every step of the way, no matter how long it took, but maybe I was being naïve. Maybe we needed to start facing up to the fact that Tadgh might not wake up, or he might wake up a different version of the Tadgh we knew.

'I met Greg in the corridor,' I said to Senan. 'Sarah went into labour in the storm. The babies are in the NICU.'

'God, that's awful. How is she?' Senan asked.

'Greg said they're all doing good. The babies are very premature but they're doing well.'

'What did they have?'

'Would you believe, I forgot to ask?' I said, mortified. 'Greg must have thought I was so rude, but my head is all over the place right now.'

I reached out across the bed and held Tadgh's hand. Suddenly I was sure I felt his fingers curl around mine, but the movement was so gentle, it was more of a brush against my skin. I instantly looked up at his face, but it was expressionless.

I turned to Senan. 'I think I just felt him squeeze my hand – I mean, it was very light, but I don't think I imagined it...' I began to feel unsure of myself. Perhaps it had just been wishful thinking.

Senan jumped up and moved closer to Tadgh's head. 'Tadgh,' he called. 'Can you hear me, Tadgh? It's Senan.'

Tadgh's eyelids flickered. Although his eyes didn't open, I knew he could hear what we were saying.

'He can hear us!' Senan cried.

'Tadgh, it's me, Penny,' I tried.

His eyelids continued to twitch, and I knew he was listening to us.

'It's okay, Tadgh, take as long as you need. We'll be right here for you when you're ready to wake up.'

Suddenly, as if he was summoning all his strength, his eyes opened, and he began to look around.

'Tadgh!' we shouted. 'You're awake!'

'You stayed,' Tadgh croaked,

I laughed as sheer joy at hearing his voice filled my heart. Senan and I grinned manically at each other before hugging one another tightly.

'I did, Tadgh, and I will never leave you again,' I said, reaching for his hand as tears began coursing freely down my face. 'Ever.'

BOOKS BY IZZY BAYLISS

The Lily McDermott Series

The Girl I was Before
Baked with Love

The Inishbeg Cove Series

The Secrets of Inishbeg Cove
Coming Home to Inishbeg Cove
Escape to Inishbeg Cove

A LETTER FROM IZZY

Thank you so very much for reading *Coming Home to Inishbeg Cove,* I adored writing this story especially because it was written in the middle of a pandemic and it provided a welcome distraction during a turbulent year. Although the village of Inishbeg Cove is a fictional place, it is inspired by lots of tiny fishing villages dotted along Ireland's beautiful wild Atlantic way. If you enjoyed the story and would like to keep up-to-date with my latest releases, you can sign up to my newsletter on www.izzybayliss.com. I promise never to spam you and you can unsubscribe at any time.

If you enjoyed *Coming Home to Inishbeg Cove*, then I would really appreciate if you could leave a short review on Amazon. Reviews really help to get a book noticed by Amazon who will then promote it to new readers, so they are hugely important to us authors. It doesn't have to be long – just one line will do – and I will be very grateful.

Thank you for reading.
    Love, Izzy x

ACKNOWLEDGMENTS

Firstly, I have to thank my ever-supportive family, my husband Simon and our four children Lila, Tom, Bea & Charlie who are my 'home'.

I must also thank my dear friend and fellow author Janelle Brooke Harris for always being there with a listening ear and for keeping me sane.

To Richie in More Visual who designed my cover and was able to capture my vision so easily. It was a pleasure working with you.

Also, to Jane Hammett Editing Services for your eagle eye.

I also owe a huge thank you to the amazingly supportive blogger community who have been so supportive of my books. I am always amazed at the enthusiasm you have and am grateful for all that you do helping us authors to spread the word.

Lastly, thank you to you the reader. From all the titles out there that you could pick from, thank you for choosing my book. I hope you enjoyed it!

Izzy xx

ABOUT THE AUTHOR

Izzy Bayliss lives in Ireland with her husband and four young children and their hyperactive puggle. A romantic at heart, she loves nothing more than cosying up in front of the fire with a good book. **Coming Home to Inishbeg Cove** is the second book in the Inishbeg Cove series.

You can find out more about Izzy Bayliss on www.izzybayliss.com.

She can also be found hanging about on Facebook @izzybaylissauthor or Twitter @izzybayliss.

She also writes emotional women's fiction as Caroline Finnerty.